# ONCE UPO

## Delilah Street Urban Fantasy Novels

## Midnight Louie, PI, mystery novels

**Once Upon A Midnight Noir**
Copyright December 2012 © Carole Nelson Douglas
All rights reserved
ISBN-10: 0-9744742-3-1
ISBN-13: 978-0-9744742-3-6

"The Riches There That Lie" from *Poe's Lighthouse*
Copyright © 2007

"Bogieman" from *Unusual Suspects*
Copyright © 2008

"Butterfly Kiss" from *The Mammoth Book of Vampire Romance* Copyright © 2008

Proofreader: Pat Martin
Images Copyright iStock.com
Cover, interior covers and book design © by Carole Nelson Douglas
Author photo © by Sam Douglas

# Praise for Midnight Louie
# and Delilah Street

# ONCE UPON
# A MIDNIGHT NOIR

Three slightly paranormal stories
by

## CAROLE NELSON DOUGLAS

## A WISHLIST BOOK
http://www.wishlistpublishing.com

For the real and original Midnight Louie and all
the rescue cats in homes everywhere, and for
their  compassionate companions

## TABLE OF CONTENTS

# INTRODUCTION

These two stories and a novella blending paranormal and mystery elements link two very different Las Vegas PIs from two series. The noir urban fantasy series features Delilah Street, Paranormal Investigator, and the long-running Midnight Louie contemporary mystery series has four human protagonists, but includes chapters relating the parallel investigations of a black alley cat who's a hard-boiled feline sleuth. *Mostly Murder* called Midnight Louie's narration "an irresistible combination of Sam Spade and Nathan Detroit" that invokes classic gumshoe, Damon Runyon of *Guys and Dolls*, and Mrs. Malaprop.

The collection's opening story, "Bogieman," introduces Delilah Street's Vegas of supernatural power brokers, like the albino rock star who owns the Inferno hotel, and such tourist attractions as film noir characters called CinSims (cinema simulacrums). Humphrey Bogart as gumshoe Sam Spade is one of them and his immortal form seems to have been… murdered. Can the actor affectionately known as 'Bogie' really die?

In "Butterfly Kiss," Midnight Louie, invokes his feline mystical side to visit Delilah's alternative Vegas and discovers a dying vampire and his devoted companion cat. With Delilah as lead detective, the pair set out to unmask the would-be murderer among the genteel vampire's blood suppliers: he survives by taking a little from a lot. Which of his clients wants to kill him? And will Louie survive a feline fatale who can really get her hooks into him?

"The Riches There That Lie" takes its title from an Edgar Allan Poe poem. This Midnight Louie story appeared in an anthology in which many authors made a fragment of an unfinished Poe tale into a story in their own style. I was asked to do a Louie story, so wrote about his Past Life Adventure on a spooky and isolated lighthouse in the North Sea shortly after the French Revolution.

The Poe fragment starts this last section, so readers can see how it became a Midnight Louie tale.

# THE FIRST TALE

BOGIEMAN

A DELILAH STREET STORY

CAROLE NELSON DOUGLAS

**Sam Spade's splayed** body was a symphony in black and white on the hellfire-orange carpet of the Inferno Hotel.

It had that pale and wan look down pat. His skin was ashen, his hair and beard stubble gray, his suit pinstriped in silver and dark charcoal, the nearby fedora a soft gray. Only his eyebrows and hatband were black.

So. Who would want to kill Sam Spade?

Who would want to kill Humphrey Bogart, for that matter?

And, legally, could either one of them be murdered?

Here's the deal. This is Las Vegas, after all. I live and work here. Delilah Street, PI. That's PI as in Paranormal Investigator. Lucky me.

A lot of this Alt-Vegas of the early twenty-first century is unlucky, including the pervasive presence of all the unhumans released by the Millennium Revelation. Instead of Apocalypse Now at the Turn,

1

we got Apocalypse Now and Forever. The 2000-year millennium didn't bring the vaunted end of the world, but the end of the world as we knew it. All the legendary bogeymen and women of history and myth showed up, maybe not exactly as advertised in our nightmares, but there. Witches and werewolves and zombies, oh, my!

Sam Spade sprang from the black type on white paper Dashiell Hammett had rolled through his manual typewriter almost a hundred years ago. Humphrey Bogart had been a human actor, but dead for almost sixty years, since 1957.

Add a little high-tech enterprise to exploit the new supernatural population, and you had what lay before me, either dead or merely unplugged: one of the fabulous Las Vegas CinSims.

The CinSim that lay immobile on the carpet was an amalgam of character and actor that had been moving and "living" until person or persons unknown—or *un*persons unknown—had driven a corkscrew from the Inferno Bar into its all-too-solid chest.

And there was yet a third persona present, last but not least. That would be whoever's resurrected dead body had been the medium upon which the silver screen icon, Humphrey Bogart, who played Sam Spade in the 1941 film classic, *The Maltese Falcon*, had been recreated.

The corkscrew spiraled into the dead man's chest, but was an ordinary mortal weapon capable of killing a CinSim? That word is short for Cinema Simulacrum, and this town was teaming with them. They had been reanimated, certainly, but were they capable of dying? Of being murdered?

And why was I standing here contemplating all these unknowns?

Because besides being Delilah Street, Paranormal Investigator, I'm a silver medium. I have an unexplained affinity for any kind of silver…the sterling kind in jewelry, mirror backings, mercury glass, and the silver nitrate that was used in black-and-white film strips, from which the CinSim personas are stripped.

CinSims are the billion-dollar baby of a literal Industrial Light and Magic post-Spielberg special effects company. They exist by mating a complex copyright network that leases the Silver Screen characters to entertainment venues, with the grave-robbers employed by the Immortality Mob to provide the flesh-and-bone "canvas" on which the animated effect is achieved.

Smuggling zombies into the U.S. is against the law. Once they get here and disappear into their CinSim overlay, they're just hard-to-trace illegal aliens, like ordinary live border-crossers.

It's no coincidence that most of the zombies are imported from Mexico.

CinSims are one of latter-day Las Vegas's most enduringly popular attractions—wouldn't you like to shoot the breeze with John Wayne as the Ringo Kid or Bette Davis as Jezebel?—and the city's most morally ambiguous creations.

I knew and liked a lot of CinSims around town, and the feeling was mutual. Yeah, CinSims have feelings, which almost nobody bothers to find out. They make terrific snitches. Everyone treats them like trained dogs it's safe to talk in front of. We get along because I treat them like real people. So I mourned Sam Spade/Humphrey Bogart, even though we'd never met.

"Okay, Miss Street. There's not much to see. What do you think?" The voice was brusque. This bizarre case, the first dead CinSim ever, had brought out the Las Vegas Metropolitan Police Department's captain of homicide, Kennedy Malloy. "Getting any useful 'vibes' off the so-called body?" her surprisingly lilting voice asked.

Kennedy Malloy was not a man. Yeah, I thought that too when I first heard the name. I first heard the name from my sudden personal interest and sometimes professional partner, Ricardo Montoya, ex-FBI guy and secret dowser for the dead. He was good at dowsing a lot of things, including me. Ric was the zombie expert, but he was consulting in Juarez. Malloy had been a professional pal of his until

I came along and snagged the benefits. She still was his friend. And no friend of mine.

"You're supposed to have this rapport with the CinSims," she was saying now, a trim blond with hazel eyes and the hard-edged moxie of women moving up in a man's profession.

"Usually they're alive," I said. "Or at least moving and talking, like the motion pictures that spawned them."

"I'm giving you two hours. You'll have to deal with the various entities that 'own' the remains. They came out like maggots the minute this was called in. Then we cart this...'star stuff' away. We'll call the metropolitan waste department. I don't see what an autopsy could do. The body's already long dead. It'll stink soon, for sure. And burial doesn't seem necessary."

Behind her, Nick Charles—like Sam Spade another Dashiell Hammett creation—known as the Thin Man for the title of his first novelistic case, clucked his teeth.

"It isn't nice for a public servant to disrespect discriminated-against minorities," he said.

Malloy spun on him. "A bleeding-heart like Street here can go all gooey over this character running out of film, but you CinSims have no civil rights in this town or this country. You're all copyrighted and leased entertainment entities."

5

"At *least*," Nick Charles said in his slightly soused but shrewd way, "somebody cared enough to copyright us. I don't see a Kennedy Malloy Barbie in *your* future, captain."

I swallowed a giggle. Nick Charles was from back in the day—the nineteen-thirties—when a smart comeback was all the rage, and he still had them in...er, spades.

"I go for a gutsy modern dame," he commented to me as the captain stomped away, "but one with a clever lip on her as well as looks, like my much missed and esteemed spouse, Nora. And also the likes of you, my dear Miss Street."

"Thanks, Nicky." What a shame hotel leasing arrangements had split up as classic a noir couple as Nick and Nora Charles. Nick was a natty cinematic symphony in black tie and black-and-white all over. I sighed as I regarded the possible corpse. "Did you know this CinSim?"

"Not personally. He was attached to the Club Noir in the hotel's Lower Depths. Circle One. We are all chained to our particular 'entertainment venues', you know."

I did know. All SinCims have an internal chip that keeps them from wandering away from their home hotel or bar...or brothel.

Nicky went on after a graciously swallowed hiccup. "I can't leave this bar for the life of me. Not that I mind." He took another tipsy sip from the martini glass perpetually in hand.

"The life of me" was an ironic expression coming from his pearl-gray lips. I was maybe the only mortal who knew that the CinSims craved more freedom. A fortunate few had film histories that helped them avoid detection, so they could ditch their chip and skip out on their home assignment. Like the Invisible Man, a pal of Nicky's, and therefore of mine.

I was particularly fond of Nick Charles, not only for his jazz-age detective history, but because his "cousin"—both played by the same long-dead actor, William Powell—was my boss's "man Godfrey" from another film of the thirties. My boss was Hector Nightwine, producer of the Las Vegas and beyond-set *CSI: Crime Scene Instincts* TV series that had been the rage since God made maggots and a profit motive.

It still astounded me that various versions of roles played by the same actor had been resurrected as utterly individual SinCims. Even now, as we contemplated the death of this Sam Spade incarnation, I remembered that Humphrey Bogart was alive in some Hemingway novel made into film at a hotel down the Strip.

"I would have never given up Mary Astor," Nicky mused, speaking of the actress who played *The*

*Maltese Falcon*'s femme fatale. "A good-looker and really classy dame. What's a little deception between film noir lovers?"

That's when it occurred to me. A *CinSim* could have offed Sam Spade. Say, Mary Astor playing Brigid O'Shaunessy, the woman who loved Sam Spade…he'd turned her in to the police in *The Maltese Falcon*. Say that greedy kingpin, Gutman, the "Fat Man" from the film. Lots of these animated characters are actors who were alive and semi-well in Las Vegas long after the movies were made. Who was to say cinematic loves and hates didn't transfer with their portrayals?

But the prime problem was who had been killed: the zombie body, the film character applied over it, or the actor who'd originated the film role?

Only God can make a tree, but these days, man could make, and remake, anything. Including original sin, the first murder of a CinSim.

**I didn't relish** interviewing the interested parties leaning against the bar with its fire-lizard aquarium base that resembled a scene of capering devils in Hell.

I recognized the lawyer for the Immortality Mob from the way he clutched his faux crocodile briefcase. He was overdressed for Vegas's dessert climate in a gray sharkskin suit and vintage Op Art tie. The Incorporated FX and Magic Show technician who fine-tunes and places the CinSims lounged beside him, long-haired, laid-back, and wearing tattooed blue jeans.

The third figure was the Inferno's head honcho, a rock superstar I'd both tangled and tangoed with. Cocaine was an updated, albino Elvis in tight white leather pants, long white hair, and mirror shades. No one quite knew what he was—vampire, fallen angel, con man CEO—besides sexy.

I was an ex-TV reporter, so I sashayed right over.

"Miss Delilah Street," Cocaine said in his belly-tightening bass voice. His stage costume included a flowing white poet's shirt open to his navel. Despite having just finished a two-hour show, his albino skin was dry as a bone. No one had ever seen him sweat. No one had ever seen his eyes, either. I didn't care to. Ever.

"Who owns the body?" I asked.

"Just what we were discussing," the dead-croc hugger said. "I'm Peter Eddy, the intellectual property rights attorney for IFX-MS, Industrial Special Effects and Magic Show. Mr. Cocaine here is refusing to let our technician download what's left of the persona into his computer. And the police captain has been none too friendly either."

"Police captains aren't promoted to be friendly. Any suspects?"

"None." Eddy shuddered at the very idea. "An unfortunate accident. The CinSim must have fallen on a bar implement. Perhaps it was drinking. The technicians can't control their every move. Yet."

I eyed the tech guy. "Aren't they chained to their venues? This guy should have never left the Club Noir level to come up here."

"Absolutely right." His hands with their bitten-to-the-quick nails smoothed the small, unmarked silver case slung over his shoulder.

"Your name is?" I always like a full cast of suspects.

"Reggie Owens. Our program prevents unauthorized wanderings. Someone must have hacked into the programming to move him here. I could upload Bogart and Spade right now, and let the police and Mr. Eddy dispose of the Z-canvas, but Mr. Christophe won't okay it."

"Christophe" was Cocaine's supposed real name, first and last, but the fans in the mosh pit screamed themselves hoarse begging for their drug of choice by the nickname they gave him. His friends called him Snow, and so did I, even though I wasn't exactly a friend. Call me a thorn in the side.

I lifted an interrogatory eyebrow in his direction.

"Nobody," he said, "is disabling an Inferno Hotel CinSim on my premises. I want to know who offed it, and how and why. And I want Miss Street to do the job."

Goodie. Put me on the hot seat between three quarreling superpowers in Las Vegas. I decided to let them fight over the retread corpse and excused myself to hunt up any possible witnesses.

Nick Charles was lighting a cigarette for a willowy woman in sleek Nora Charles evening velvet. He had quite a following at the Inferno Bar. Like Snow, the CinSims had their devoted fans. Called CinSymbs, for CinSim Symbiants—yes, if you're good at tongue-twisters, this is your subculture—they dressed in silk velvet vintage clothes, but in black and white, including their clown-white made-up skin and vamp-black dyed hair.

"Thanks, Nicky," the sexy probable platinum blond said, patting her pale gray hair in a weird, grandmotherly way.

He turned to me with relief.

"Now that we're alone, what did you see?" I asked him.

"The bar was mobbed from the Seven Deadly Sins performance, with a monster mash of Cocaine groupies, the usual CinSymbs doing both the rock concert and the bar scene, tourists milling around with their plugged-in communication cameras. Drugs, sex, and rock and roll. A little gin was all it took to get high in my day, and the sex came without that blaring musical accompaniment. Maybe just a little Noel Coward."

"And a *lot* of gin in your case, Nicky."

"Guilty. But not of this CinSim's current condition."

"You don't say 'dead'?"

"It's debatable, isn't it? The…personage was discovered when the crowd began to thin after the Sins concert. Just there." He pointed.

"Had you ever seen him before?"

"No, but I knew of him. He was the coming thing, with that tough guy stuff. No white tie and tails and smooth patter for him. And it was ironic that Sam Spade was portrayed by an actual swell like Bogart, who'd been expelled from a fancy Eastern prep school. Film can be fickle."

I lowered my voice. "Are you aware of other CinSims leaving their, um, moorings."

"Well, our Invisible friend gets around."

I checked the neighboring empty barstools for a betraying depression in the middle, but they were all undimpled red leather.

"Not tonight," Nick said, sipping from his martini glass. "Not that I know of. I was distracted, of course," His pleasantly hazy eyes sharpened. "It's as if the body was planted here. When the crowd parted like the Red Sea, *voila!* Somebody wanted it to be found, and publicly."

I accepted what Nicky offered: the Albino Vampire cocktail I'd invented from white chocolate liqueur and vanilla vodka to piss off Snow. He hated the rumor he was a vampire. Resistance was futile. Snow had merely appropriated my cocktail creation for the bar, since I'd used his ingredients, and made a mint.

While I sipped and thought, I felt a sharp bite on my rear. No, the barstools didn't have teeth and claws. The Invisible Man was announcing his presence. Being Invisible, he hadn't had a date since the nineteen-forties and pinching unsuspecting women was his kick. Since he'd once saved my life, I put up with his idea of a pick-up line.

"I knew," he whispered in my ear, "Sam was going to make a run for it. Humphrey was hankering to visit another venue."

"You saw him get to the bar area?" I mumbled to my glass rim. The tourist dame next to me with the cigarette gave me an "Are you nuts?" glance.

"Hell, I helped him get off Circle One," the Invisible Man mumbled. "He mixed with the CinSymbs up here, blended right in. I lost him until Nick and everyone saw him frozen on the floor when the crowd cleared. Talk about a 'still' life."

"Why the corkscrew?"

"I don't have the faintest, Miss Street. *Umm*, you smell good."

"It's not me, it's my Albino Vampire."

"How naughty of Christophe to rip you off like that. You want me to put quinine in his onstage bottled water?"

I shook my head, getting another Look from the woman on my right.

"Can I have a sip?" the Invisible Man cajoled.

"I guess." I watched the smooth white liquid in my martini glass descend an inch. "Sip?"

"*Umhmm*, good. They never feed or water me. The corkscrew? I don't know. Someone hurled a switchblade at me once. It stuck, but it didn't hurt, and it didn't do any damage. It was like it hit corkboard. These borrowed bodies are sturdy."

"How'd they manage to make you invisible?"

"It comes with the character, not the canvas." I felt a white chocolate buss on the cheek. "'Bye, baby." Sweet.

I glanced at the triumvirate with ownership interests in the Bogart/Spade CinSim. The lawyer and the techie were sweating bullets, but Snow seemed cool as an ice cube. I ambled over to eavesdrop.

"While you let this Street woman pretend to investigate, I don't trust the police to guard our property," lawyer Eddy told Snow. "Some of these rubber-necking tourists might violate our copyright and tear away pieces of its clothing."

True, the crime scene was surrounded by tourists five-feet deep, not to mention the Inferno's hovering airborne flock of mirror-ball security cameras the size of grapefruits.

Cocaine/Christophe sighed and reached up to the pink ruby-dotted black leather collar circling his dead-white neck. He pressed a faceted black gemstone separating the rubies.

"I'll have Grizelle, my head of security. watch the…er, canvas…while I escort Miss Street to the CinSim's home environment."

The tourists parted with *oohs* of anxious wonder. A six-hundred-pound white tiger with green eyes stalked past the people and the police CSI crew to stand by the body. They all moved back. Way back.

"Nicky," Snow said. "Get the gentlemen some drinks while I escort Miss Street below."

"Charmed," Nick Charles turned to the two IFX-MS guys. "I recommend gin. And gin. And gin. Which would you like, sir? A gin rickey? Martini? Gimlet?"

"You checked your security satellites?" I asked Snow as we moved away. He was an Invisible Man himself once offstage. I don't know how he managed it, but he avoided being mobbed. Some things you don't want to know in post-Millennium Revelation Las Vegas. I had my secrets too.

"Checked them immediately. The crowd around the bar was too thick to isolate anyone. Whatever stopped Sam Spade cold, it happened during my…er, curtain call."

Except there was no curtain, just the band drawn back onstage by clapping, hooting, digital screams. I could picture every eye fixed onstage as he bent down to uplift a dozen lucky, screaming female fans for what they called the Brimstone Kiss. It wasn't just a hasty smooch, either. Perfect timing for distracting notice from an unprecedented murder.

"You know you won't win custody in court," I told Snow as we headed toward the roaring dragon's mouth that housed the elevators to the Inferno Hotel's lower depths. "You're just a leasee. And no one will claim the anonymous, illegally resurrected body."

"Sure this isn't your FBI friend Ric's work?"

"Ex-FBI. And Ric dowses for the dead, he doesn't create them. Nor does he trifle with the resurrected Dead like you Vegas moguls do."

The brushed stainless steel doors opened between flaming jaws seven feet wide and high. I admit to a tremor. I'd never been below the Inferno's main floor, which was bad enough.

In the elevator, Snow tilted his head back against the stainless-steel-mirror walls.

"This is important, Delilah. My people are my people, CinSims or not. No one messes with me and mine. Not even you. Find whoever, or whatever, did this. I'll handle the cops and the corporations."

"Haven't you got 'people' to do that? Attorneys, muscle?"

"I run a hands-on operation."

I was sure the eyes behind those glossy black lenses were giving me a lazy and provocative half-stare.

Or maybe they were eyeing the Elsa Peretti sapphire-studded sterling silver bangle on my left wrist. I can't afford that high-end sort of bracelet, but silver is a sort of familiar of mine. This particular piece of it had a literal lock on me, having started out as a lock of Snow's angel-white hair. It changed from weapon to bond to bling and migrated all over my body. I'd touched the damn strand Snow sent me because it reminded me of my white Lhasa apso dog, Achilles, lost to a vampire bite. He bit the vampire, mind you, but died of blood poisoning. Or maybe not. He kept turning up alive in my dreams. Anyway, my weakness for Achilles had led to having Snow's creepy lock of hair as a permanent fashion accessory-cum-martial arts attachment.

"Besides," he was saying, "I didn't want to miss the opportunity of working with you."

"Why? You know I despise you and all your works."

"That's why. You're totally objective."

"Just show me where the dead CinSim was supposed to be."

"This level is all key clubs," he said, waiting for me to exit the flaming dragon's mouth on Circle

One. I knew what that meant. The first of the nine circles of Hell from Dante's *Inferno*.

"Fantasy enviros," Snow went on, proud of his hellfire clubs. "Club Noir offers all the famous names and faces from the era. Here's *The Maltese Falcon* boutique hotel and bistro. Please don't be hard on Peter Lorre; he gets kicked around enough in the film."

By then we'd entered a pair of etched glass double doors bearing the film's name. Beyond them lay a moving wax museum of movie moments: walls playing the famous scenes in 3-D, the reel characters moving around, mumbling lines, intermixing with real-life visitors to Vegas who'd paid for the privilege.

Peter Lorre as Joel Cairo caught my eye, and scuttled away. He didn't know much in the film and he wouldn't know much now. Snow was right. He was too pathetic to bother with, and so Sam Spade had also determined.

"I'm bad," Mary Astor as Bridgid O'Shaughnessy was breathing at a fat man in a Hawaiian shirt and baggy shorts. "I'm so bad."

I'd seen at a glance that Bogie was missing from the scenery, so I stepped into Mary's barside seduction scene.

"Get lost, tourist," I said. The guy bristled, but obeyed. "So did you do in Sam?" I asked Bridgid.

"Who are you to ask questions like that? You're not in the script."

"Neither was an offed Sam Spade. When did you last see him?"

"Sam? Dead? It can't be?"

"It is. 'Fess up, sister. You know you had the hots for him and he was ready to send you up river on a murder rap. Why wouldn't you drive a corkscrew into his chest if you had a chance?"

"No! I loved him. I'd never kill him."

"Seems like you set him up a few times, for just that result."

"That was the script! I had to do it. I hated the ending. Sam would never have sold me out. He didn't give a toot about his partner, Miles Archer. He'd been screwing Archer's wife, Iva, but then he met and loved me. He really loved me. The scriptwriters messed us up. Why don't you ask Iva where she was when Sam got corkscrewed?"

Good point. I racked my brain for the cast list from the film. Snow stepped into the scene, a hand-held computer showing just what I'd wanted.

"Thanks, Jeeves." I was getting into the fact that maybe he really needed me to solve this. If that entitled me to hand him some lip without personal peril, it was pretty sweet.

Okay. Iva Archer. Miles Archer had been Sam Spade's partner until he was killed. Iva had been the femme fatale in the threesome until Bridgid O'Shaughnessy had shown up. Was Sam Spade's "death" today part of the backstory mayhem of *The Maltese Falcon* novel and film?

I found Iva having a hasty talk with Peter Lorre/Joel Cairo. She was a refined beauty for a cheap PI's wife.

"Sam Spade has left the building," I told her. The Elvis reference meant nothing, but her face turned a whiter shade of pale gray.

"I don't know what you're talking about," she told me. "I live here. I'm a widow, don't you know that? Who'd walk out on a widow? Sam wouldn't leave me. Don't you say that he would!"

Women in film noir sure were hair-trigger. "Okay, okay. I just wanted to talk to him. I have a case."

She eyed me. "Yeah, you dames have 'cases,' all right." She looked around. Looked harder. No Sam Spade to be found. "Get outa here! You're crazy."

I backed off, but I didn't stop considering which one of these fictional characters made flesh would want to kill the leading man, even if he was a hard-boiled son-of-a-gun who'd send his new sweetheart to the pen. And how had someone lured him out of his safe, scripted environment for a date with death in the Inferno Bar?

I left *The Maltese Falcon* enviro, Snow at my side.

"This is complicated," I said.

"This is Las Vegas."

I glanced around at the double-doored entries to many cinema worlds. We were in a freaking CinSim multiplex!

"Is this an all-Bogart level?" I asked.

"No. All noir. Only two of the clubs center on Bogart."

"*Casablanca?*"

"My favorite. You want to see?'

Snow, hooked on true love and self-sacrifice? Sell me another bridge in Brooklyn.

"You must like the hot, dry Moroccan climate," I hazarded.

"Hot is my sexual preference."

"It was Satan's too." We went through another frosted glass pair of doors into Rick's *Café Américan* Bar.

Bogie was here, in a slightly wilted white evening jacket, leaning over an upright piano on which a black guy played "As Time Goes By." Customers in Bermuda shorts and Hawaiian shirts looked a lot more at home here. Ingrid Bergman sat alone at a table, looking pensive while being chatted up by two surfer dudes. And Peter Lorre lurked around the fringes, having again played the same conniving, cringing lowlife he was so good at in *The Maltese Falcon*.

I ankled over, and his beady eyes lit up. He wasn't used to women seeking him out.

"Hi, cutie, can I buy you a gin rickey?" I didn't even know what a gin rickey was, except it evoked the name of the bar's fictional owner…and of my own personal cutie, Ric Montoya, come to think of it.

He would have looked good here at Rick's place. Much better-looking than Bogart.

"You can buy me some information," I said, melding into forties noir-speak. "Have there been any attempts on Rick's life lately?"

"This is Casablanca. If the local occupying Nazis aren't after you the international rat pack is. Rick can take care of himself." Lorre eyed Bergman. "That dame is no good for him. That's the kind of classy dame even a hard-headed guy could lose his sense of self-preservation over."

"He did," I said. "Do you ever trespass on your 'cousin's' scenario in the next club over?"

"Never! We are forbidden to meet. It's not in our contracts."

"Aren't you even tempted?"

"No. He's a weasely little rat who will never get the girl. Here, I get to talk to you, cutie."

"Not any more."

I looked around for Snow. He was hanging over the top of the small, white upright piano, singing along to Sam's soulful rendition of "As Time Goes By." I suppose even a rock star harbors visions of crooning classics.

On the "a kiss is just a kiss," he turned those blind-man glasses my way.

*A kiss is just a kiss, my eye!* His Brimstone Kiss after the show addicted the clamoring mosh-pit females to a repeat performance that would never happen. These pathetic Cocaine junkies attended every performance, living their lives only to support their doomed habit. I was secretly working to rehabilitate them, for my own reasons.

"We done here?" I asked as I walked over.

He finished crooning the phrase. Then, since the fundamentals still apply, he escorted me to the Circle One lobby.

"Got any ideas?" he asked.

"Just a couple more questions."

He waited.

"The CinSims are strictly tied to their performance areas, right?"

"Theoretically. It depends how diligent the hotelier is about keeping a leash on them."

"And you?"

"I'd find it more interesting it they *would* depart from the script. Call me contrary, but tourists like the unexpected."

"So you don't have them tied down as tightly as some."

"No."

"And Sam Spade might have gotten up to the Inferno Bar on his own."

"If he'd had the will. That's the intriguing part. Does a CinSim have free will?"

"Humans do."

"They seem to think so."

"And an unhuman like you?"

"Are you certain I'm unhuman, or what kind of unhuman I might be?"

The rumor said master vampire. I wasn't so sure. "No. That's your devilish charm."

I doubt many people made Snow laugh, but I did then.

"That's *my* devilish charm," I said.

But he didn't answer, only reached down and snapped his forefinger on my bracelet, my bond, his former lovelock, making it chime.

"What else did you want to know?" he asked.

"Which other hotels host Bogart SinCims, and what incarnation they use."

"Easy. My office computer has stats on all the competition."

**On the way** back up in the elevator, the pink ruby collar buzzed. His forefinger stabbed the black onyx stone.

"The police and interested CinSim parties are getting restless, boss," came a deep, growly voice.

"Keep them busy. I'll want them in my office in a bit. We may have something for them soon."

I was indignant. " 'We', white man?" Well, he was literally white from crown to toe, as far as I know, or ever wish to know.

"You've got an idea on this CinSim murder, haven't you?" he asked.

"Yes. Maybe you can just read my mind and take it."

"Maybe I like you working for a living."

Me, too. I'd been an unemployed TV reporter until this paranormal investigator gig evolved. Actually, I enjoyed working for someone other than Hector Nightwine, my landlord and somewhat ghoulish mentor.

Snow's office sported a lot of glossy black furniture and a huge tufted white leather executive chair.

Even the laptop computer case was glossy black.

I saw myself, darkly, in its reflective surface while his pale hands with the china-white fingernails punched keys and scrolled and hunted.

"All right," he said at last. "The Gehenna has the only other Bogart film leased."

"To *Have and to Have Not*, right?"

"Is that a proposal or a question?"

I made a face. I always knew that Snow had designs on me. I just didn't know what for. Or why.

"Not one of Hemingway's best novels," he said. "Or Bogart's best roles."

"Can I see the screen?"

He spun the laptop to face me.

I started punching my own buttons, looking up the original cast and the reviewer notes.

*Aha!*

That film had debuted Bogart's future wife, long, lean teenage model Lauren Bacall, and had made them into "Bogie and Bacall" for eternity. Her character in the movie was even nicknamed "Slim." That was the film where she'd taunted the Bogart character that he knew how to whistle for her, didn't he? "You just put your lips together and…blow."

It's amazing what passed for racy seventy-some years ago.

"I figured out," I said, "who killed the Sam Spade CinSim. And why."

"Good."

"It's all your fault, you know."

"My fault?"

"You like your CinSims on a loose leash."

"Free will is a noble concept, especially for indentured servants."

"Sorta free will. Get Captain Malloy and the interested parties in here."

"Oh, excellent. You're going to do the pin-the-rap-on-the-perp shtick. Classic mystery finish."

I said no more, waiting.

Within ten minutes, the interested parties were herded into the room by the huge white tiger, who shifted into a skinny, six-foot-plus tall black woman with long white hair like Snow, green eyes, and red-painted nails long and sharp enough to eviscerate an adult male. She was wearing purple leather Escada and did it look good on her.

"We'll take the Inferno to court," croco-man Peter Eddy was sputtering as he took a seat, "if you deny our substantial financial interest in the now-useless CinSim."

"We'll take *you* to jail," Captain Malloy told Snow as she took her seat, "if you're ducking any wrong-doing on your part here."

Reggie, the IFX-MS technician, slouched into another leather tub-chair and shrugged his disdain for the whole inquiry. "It doesn't matter what all you honchos decide. I just need to strip our programming pronto. Then you all can fight over the remains."

"Sure you really need to deprogram the fallen CinSim?" I asked. "Let me see your portable programmer."

"No! It's IFX-MS property." He clutched the slim case to his side, but Grizelle, Snow's security chief, leaned over to slash through the leather shoulder sling with one red, tigerish claw. She slung the item down on the desk in front of me.

I tapped around and found I couldn't get anywhere without an entry code.

Everyone was watching me. Malloy was irritated. The lawyer was fixated. The tech guy was looking constipated, and who knew what Snow was thinking behind those impervious shades.

Okay. Time for a little silver medium work. These SinCims were my people, peeled from silver nitrate and given latter-day life. I let my fingers wander, like a musician. I was looking for the one right note in Sam Spade's key...a code name Sam/Humphrey would know and love.

*Effie*. The name of Spade's loyal secretary. Every private dick in those days had one. Nothing. *Iva*. Nothing. *Bridgid*. Rhymes with "frigid." Hammett named the "Fat Man" Gutman, so he was trying to tell us something. Nothing. None of the story dames registered. It had to be a woman. I tried the actress names: Mary Astor. Lee Patrick. Gladys George. Nothing.

Leather chairs creaked as representatives of three powerful forces in Las Vegas grew impatient.

Nothing from the fourth and key figure, Snow.

I entered an all-American name. Betty. Betty Bacall, before the "Lauren" became her screen moniker.

Suddenly I was in the Sam Spade file. What was left of it. Hopefully, all. *Yes!*

"You've already uploaded the Spade and Bogart personas." I looked up to accuse Reggie, the tech guy. "You erased the canvas. You stuck the dead man's chest with a redundant corkscrew to hide the fact that the canvas was already empty. Why?"

"Me? I'm only the tech zombie. I just do my job."

"The whole CinSim was right in your porta-puter all the time. You were going to *pretend* to upload the personas from the 'mysteriously' dead CinSim body. Why the subterfuge?"

Reggie squirmed in his chair, but Grizelle's red-taloned hands held him still. She leaned her face close to his and gave one of those Big Cat snarls.

"S-s-secret orders. Get this thing away from me!" Grizelle backed off her face, but not her claws. "There's nothing illegal here. No 'murder.' This CinSim was rogue. The chip told us he was trying to leave his venue. That's why I had to waste him in the Inferno Lounge. One CinSim wanders off its contracted premises, it's history, like it was before."

"Why not just withdraw the lease?"

"Too many questions. Money loss. Besides, Mr. Christophe is not a team player." He glared at our host.

I tapped some commands into the console. Up came a screenful of gobbledygook.

"Why?" Captain Malloy wanted to know. "Why get a crime scene team out here for nonsense. You can't kill a CinSim."

"Only by computer" I said. "I'm guessing the IFX-MS brass didn't want to antagonize Christophe. He's a good customer, if willful. They cancelled the contract without having to pay a kill fee. Created a mystery. A philosophical conundrum. The CinSim is indeed their property, but it was wandering and the contract hadn't run out. An executive decision. This tech man is only the hired hand who did the take-down."

Captain Kennedy arched a pale eyebrow. "Not everybody can take down Sam Spade." She eyed Christophe. "You want to charge fraud?"

"I want my CinSim back. I'll say if it's out of bounds, not IFX-MS."

I spun the tech's computer across Snow's desk to face him. "Be my guest."

Captain Malloy stood. "There's no crime here. Don't call the police the next time you corporate zombie-lovers have a spat. There are some things we expect you dealers in immortality to work out for yourselves. We work the real dead beat."

She left.

The lawyer bowed out too. "It's obvious that a CinSim can't die. My job is done. You tech geeks and ghouls and girls settle it between you."

It was just the four of us. And the megabytes of Sam Spade and Humphrey Bogart.

"Your company doesn't like my operation," Snow said softly to Reggie Owens and Peter Eddy, "you come to me. You don't sneak onto my premises to off my CinSims. Got it?"

The guy was just a low-level techie. Following orders. He swallowed, glanced at Grizelle, then fled in Eddy's wake, leaving his porta-puter.

"Bogie's all here?" Snow asked me, patting it, "both role and actor?"

"I think so."

He nodded at Grizelle. She left with the computer and file, walking with one Jimmy Choo spike swaggering in front of the other, like a Big Cat stalking. Sam Spade would soon be restored to his rightful starring place in the Inferno firmament.

Snow leaned back in his infinitely programmable executive chair, running his dead white fingers through his dead white hair.

"So, Delilah. It was just unsanctioned industrial espionage. The Immortality Mob needed a comeuppance. Thanks for the quick solve. Your fee will be waiting at your cottage on Nightwine's estate."

"That may not be enough in this case."

"No? We had a deal."

"You realize why Bogie-Sam was wandering."

"He could?"

"You're a generous slave-holder, but no."

"I give them leeway. Why leave my hotel?"

"Because you don't lease Betty Bacall."

"What? You're saying he needed a girlfriend?"

"I'm saying Bogie needed his wife."

Snow was silent, taking in all the implications. Then he sat up, wired. "The CinSims want a life? Real life?"

"Why not? They're a blend of actor and role…" I shrugged.

"They're a blend of actor and role," he repeated, "and corporeal canvas."

"Exactly, but the role is written. The actor has a soul. Humphrey Bogart wanted to replay the part that united him with the woman he loved in the real world."

"Lauren Bacall, not her character in the film, 'Slim' Browning?"

I nodded. "I wouldn't expect someone like you to understand."

"I understand that this is a most…interesting development. More interesting than IFX-MS's tawdry attempt to confuse the issues with a phony homicide."

"I agree."

"I'll have to pay a bundle for the *Casablanca* cast. Ingrid Bergman was a much bigger star than Mary Astor. The Gehenna will want more for *To Have and to Have Not* and Lauren Bacall. On the other hand, I always thought she was a classy dame."

"Noir does not become you, Snow. And while you're arranging for new CinSims, I have a suggestion."

"Suggestion?"

"Demand."

"And you want—?"

"Given the smidgeon of soul you've now discovered in the CinSims, I think, at the least, that Nick Charles deserves a *Nora* Charles at the Inferno bar."

"What a romantic you are, Delilah Street. And pretty pricey yourself." Snow made a note on the laptop. "I'll look into a Myrna Loy/Nora Charles lease in the morning. I suppose you want the damn dog too?"

My hand unconsciously went to the damned silver bracelet, once a lock of Snow's hair as white and supple as my lost Lhasa apso's floor-length coat. I nodded.

"And Asta, the wire-haired terrier," Snow said as he typed, long, white fingers playing the keyboard like a piano. "One dead dog, coming up."

Didn't I wish.

**AUTHOR'S NOTE**: This is the first Delilah Street short story. It was written for the ***UNUSUAL SUSPECTS*** urban fantasy short story anthology edited by mystery author Dana Stabenow, and introduces her post-paranormal apocalypse Las Vegas. Here werewolves are hotel-casino mobsters, vampires ancient and post-modern have very different...tastes, and horror and film noir characters live again as CinSims, cinema simulacrums.

Animal lovers, don't despair. Since so many characters in Delilah's world have some supernatural mojo, I wouldn't bet that Delilah's lost little white Lhasa Apso dog, Achilles, won't be found quite alive...somewhere, somehow. Meanwhile, Delilah's rescued a paranormally talented 150-pound wolf-wolfhound cross dog she names Quicksilver in the first of five Delilah Street novels so far.

## Delilah Street, Paranormal Investigator novels

*Dancing with Werewolves*

*Brimstone Kiss*

*Vampire Sunrise*

*Silver Zombie*

*Virtual Virgin*

# THE SECOND TALE

# BUTTERFLY KISS

## DELILAH STREET
## AND MIDNIGHT LOUIE
two paranormal detectives
meet a dying vampire

# CAROLE NELSON DOUGLAS

**The name is** Louie, Midnight Louie. I like my night life shaken, not stirred.

A veteran PI can never know his home turf's dark side well enough, and I have padded the neon-lit Strip of Las Vegas and its byways and backways for a long time.

Vegas has always been known as Sin City, but the "Sin" part has gotten a lot deadlier since the Millennium Revelation at the turn of the twenty-first century revealed some of the bloodsuckers in Vegas were actually supernatural—such as vampires, and werewolves.

I admit that I am not *au courante*, so to speak, with all the varieties of crime and punishment on the paranormal side of the street. So I have made it my business tonight to leave the Las Vegas of my normal, nonsupernatural existence (as if Vegas could ever be "normal") and find an entrance to that local nomadic subterranean pit dedicated to the dark side of sin called the Sinkhole.

Given the so-called "mystical" side of my kind, it is easy to slip into the paranormal underworld. I am not impressed. Sure, the full moon is putting on a show topside, so I must dodge werewolves in the street, but I find they are mostly living La Vida Loco after their nightly blood-thirsty runs and now are only running up bills in the Sinkhole's gin joints and casinos.

Midnight Louie is light on his feet and used to keeping a low profile—a very low profile—abetted by the fact that I am short, dark, and handsome. My thick black pelt blends into the night, except for my baby greens, which can emit a demonic crimson glow when the few street lights hit them.

My kind has had a bad rep since witches were burned at the stake. I find that useful in my work. In fact, a tourist couple happens to notice me and runs the other way, shrieking that I must not cross their paths.

Fine with me, folks. Your footwear bears an odor of bunions. Or is that "onions" from a zombie burger joint?

All around me echo the same sounds of merriment and debauchery you get in mainstream Vegas, interspersed with occasional screams, growls, and moans.

Then I catch an aroma that perks my wing flaps and tingles my tail section.

Something feline and feminine this way comes, and it is not the shape-shifted leopard devouring a Happy Meal at the MacDungeon's across the street.

The faintest brush against my shiny satin lapels reveals a pale feathery plume tickling the hair of my chinny-chin-chin.

Wow. This first-class dame is draped in luxuriant furs, cream with crimson tips, the breed color called a flame-point. If the Sinkhole is the path to hell and this hot little number is on it, I am homeward bound!

"My name is Vesper," she breaths in my perked ear. "I have not seen you in these parts before, Big Boy."

Actually, I am. Big that is, and surely a boy. Perhaps some self-description is appropriate now that the action has turned romantic. First, I am twenty pounds of solid muscle. Check. Hairy chest, check. Concealed weapons? Check. Sixteen shivs ready to slash from my mitts and feet in a street rumble.

Best of all, I have—as they used to advertise sports cars—four on the floor and come fully equipped from the factory.

All this means I am ready, willing and able to take on any Sinkhole-dwelling humans or unhumans, and also, of course, any lone ladies requiring defensive and/or intimate maneuvers.

While I am planning the evening's escapades, the lithesome Vesper has diverted down a dim alley, only her flame-tipped train beckoning from around the corner. I hasten to follow her.

Now, any simpleton knows this is probably a trap. So do I. Not that I am a simpleton, although I am a simple fellow at heart. No, I figure I will find out what the lady *really* wants, and if it is a patsy, we will have a discussion. Either way, I intend to get to know her a lot better.

So I edge into the alley, my laser-sharp night vision kicking into full power.

Yup. Another flash of tail deep in the darkness. Classic. I slink along the dumpsters, ignoring the octopus tentacles writhing over the edges. This is no time for sushi.

Even the noise of the main drag has faded. I am invading No Man's Land. Luckily, I am no man. I have almost caught up with the elusive Vesper when I stumble across the expected trap.

It forms an unseen barrier, less than two feet high and six feet long. I peer over it only to see Vesper's eyes gleaming red in the reflected light of the street.

*Hmm,* I think to myself. We commune over a dead body. Whose? How? Why? I have my work cut out for me, I see.

Vesper hisses, baring long front fangs (so misnamed as "canine") also gleaming red in the night light. True, neon is common in Vegas, and below it. However, this looks like the sheen of blood. Could *Vesper* have killed this man?

Gorgeous as she is, she is a domestic cat. I have almost killed humans in the pursuit of my cases, but I am remarkably strong and clever. I cannot believe this bit of fluff is homicidal.

Then I reconsider. Never underestimate the female of the species, any species.

I sniff along the victim's upper torso and encounter a scent of ... nothing.

The man is not only dead, he is not ... um ... how shall I put it delicately? He is not rotting.

Now that is a truly revolting turn of events! I do scent the odd combination of earthy odors. Either this gent wore an unusual cologne or ... *aha!* My luxuriant whiskers follow the shape of a large, curved *claw* impaled near his heart.

Dainty Vesper certainly could not have wielded this large a lance.

By now someone has stumbled out of a nearby dive, leaving the rear door ajar enough to cast pale light on our tableau of three.

The deceased is indeed a young man. His dark hair contrasts a dead-white skin. He would be handsome if he had green eyes like mine, but his eyelids are closed. Vesper is rubbing back and forth on his black attire, shedding white hairs in her distress.

I realize that she has led me here. This man must have been her . . . companion. I dislike the word "owner" used in relation to my kind. I have been street-smart and fancy free since I was a kit. True, I have a human female roommate, Miss Temple Barr, a public relations expert and sometime crime-solver— with my immense help, that is—but it is a voluntary arrangement on both our parts.

Vesper releases a sad *mew* and tries to make like an ascot around the poor guy's neck. I understand the bond between human and animal, but this is over the top.

"You must remove her," a low, rasping voice says.

*Easier said than done,* I think as I whip around to see what human has arrived on the scene.

I can communicate in various ways with various members of the animal kingdom, but I do not speak to humans. This is not because I *could* not if I so wished, but, really, some of my kin have suffered much at their disloyal hands. I am not about to honor even the best of them with my voice.

As for the voice I heard, we three are still alone. No one has discovered us.

I stare at Vesper while she whimpers and buries her face in the dead guy's neck and runs her dainty muzzle along his jawline. You would think she was a Silver Screen drama queen. I am not the sentimental sort, but realize that this distraught lady must not disturb the evidence on the body.

"Vesper, no!" the faint voice says. "I will *not*. Never. Anyway, it is not enough now, and this strapping fellow you have lured here is not sufficient, either."

Midnight Louie, not sufficient? For anything? I beg your pardon. I am the primo PI in this town and have been since before God made millenniums and the Devil made brimstone. Well, so to speak.

"Go, you" the voice commands me and follows up with a demeaning order, as if I were not Midnight Louie, PI. "Scat! And consider your hide well saved. Vesper means well but this is beyond the abilities of cats."

I drop my jaw. And speak. I am not violating my vow to address no human being. This man is unhuman.

"You are still alive," I tell my handsome corpse. "For a vampire."

He coughs slightly. "Good. You hear my thoughts. My dying thoughts. My poor Vesper is offering her slender artery for my survival, but it is not enough. You must drive her away."

"Someone has staked you so you cannot move," I diagnose, on the right trail at last, now that I know the nature of the victim. The claw must be polished wood.

It is not every day—or night, I should say—that an investigator can interview the corpse, who is also a corpse-to-be even more.

"A long distance blow," he answers. "I staggered here to escape more poison wooden darts just before the curse pinned me here like a bug."

Vesper lifts her lovely throat and howls. "You good-for-nothing," she accuses me. "You have neither blood nor brains to offer! *Do something.*"

"I am a professional," I tell her. "Your fit of pique is not called for. And I am not about to trick some innocent tourist down this alley—although I could—so he or she can be drained to death."

The vampire's form stirs.

"No, no. Not to death. I am a daylight vampire, the new breed designed to mingle safely with humans. I feed on a . . . circle of willing volunteers, a mere cocktail with each, one at a time. Only now, I have been immobilized and starved. I need more than a serial filling day by day. I need a full body's blood. Keep anything human away. My will to survive could drive me to drain a person to death and make that soul into a vampire . . . one without my scruples."

I frown. "How many daylight vampires are there?"

"Only a few dozen, but the program is promising."

"Is it possible someone is trying to sabotage the movement by driving you to savagery or death?"

He gives a hollow, almost spectral laugh. "Even likely, but I do not have the time to explore that possibility, my feline friend. Can you . . . will you . . . look after Vesper when I am gone?"

Vesper emits an anguished screech and casts herself on the vampire's chest.

What can I do but promise? Still, I know I am in no position to shepherd a vampire pussycat. I need help with this case, probably human help.

**First, I** stiffen my spine and judiciously pat down the fallen vampire. He is nicely dressed in silk-blend black linen from foot to, ah, neck, and well-built as humans go under his fancy clothes. I find a couple of interesting objects in his sport coat side pockets.

One is a slick multifunction device the size of a credit card. My street-callused pads manage to punch enough buttons to call up his client list of blood donors. This causes my eyebrow whiskers to lift. They are all female, all right, and one is a well-known performer on the Strip. I could make some tidy dough from the tabloids if I outed her erotic . . . tastes.

But that would be unethical. A plan is forming in my agile brain, but things are always complicated for a guy of my physical type.

"What is this?" I ask Vesper, rolling a ping pong-ball-size object I found in his pocket from one paw to the other over the pavement.

She leaps down to swat it away from me. "My toy."

"Just a minute there." I manage to pull it safe against my hairy masculine chest. "There seems to be something inside." I perk an ear at a muted but frantic buzzing.

"*My* toy," she repeats. "My master bought it for me."

A tug of toy ensues, during which, thanks to my superior strength, the ball breaks in half like a perfectly split eggshell.

*Well.*

The buzzing, now loud enough to decipher, resolves into an indignant high-pitched voice, as the winged inhabitant gives us both what-for.

"It is a Whirr-away," Vesper says. "My master hurls it for me to chase and find."

"*Hmm.*" I trap a tiny wing under one curved claw. "I have eaten bigger mites than this by accident.

This is no 'toy,' Vesper, it is an earth-bound pixie. Very rare. Your master must treasure you indeed."

"You would stoop to petty thievery while my master lies dying?"

"I would stoop to using your 'toy' for a much more serious purpose. What is your name, little fellow?"

"I am female," the creature buzzes back at me.

"Is it true that pixies are allergic to silver?" A lot of supernaturals can be injured by silver.

I feel the tiny wing tremble against my pad. "Awful stuff. It burns my skin and if it ever enters my blood, I will die."

"Then I imagine you could spot the stuff instantly, from a long ways away?"

Another shudder. "It is far too popular as human jewelry. I smell six women wearing it on the street out there."

"What if the silver sprang from a lock of long white hair?"

The tiny human body leaps atop my mitt, pulling its wing free. "Changeling Silver. That is different. Very rare and powerful. Almost nonexistent in this realm."

"What is your name?"

"Wasp-Wing."

"I take it you can fly far and fast, Wasp-Wing."

"Like bolt lightning. I have been leashed so as not to over-challenge the vampire's feline companion."

"I usually work with a human female on my cases," I explain to all who listen, which is a fading vampire, a heart-broken vampire cat and my new pixie pal. "We need human help and I am thinking of a new partner this time who might just have the paranormal talent to do the trick. Fly topside, find the woman who wears Changeling Silver and bring her back, fast you can."

"That will depend on the woman." Wasp-Wing rustles, vanishing like a dust mote against the neon-lit night.

"My toy will never come back," Vesper mourns. "I always had to trap and fetch it."

"Nothing wins over an ally more than letting it feel useful and challenged, Vesper."

"You expect this silver-bearing human female to save my master?"

"At the very least, she can move the body."

Vesper strikes at me with fanned claws, but I easily dodge the blow. Those vampire claws may be toxic, for all I know.

"Calm down, Vesper. We all need help sometimes."

"If my master cannot drink he will die," she growls softly, curling up along his side.

I gingerly mount his chest, which of course does not lift up and down, and examine the weapon that pins him. It is a not toy either, but a curved claw two inches long. Small things can be potent, I know. Including pixies.

**Perhaps ten minutes** later, a shadow fills the alley opening, then a figure strides to our location and stands, hands on hips, feet astride, looking down. She is wearing low-rise blue jeans and a gray leotard top.

On her right elbow perches a tiny, glowing, winged figure.

"It is a good thing I brake for butterflies," she says. "My windshield almost pulverized the pixie before I discovered what it was. Am I to understand I have been summoned to perform a 'professional courtesy' for another PI?"

"Nicely put," I tell Wasp-Wing, although the woman cannot hear me.

Now that a human is on the scene, I am back to my usual handicap: my vow not to speak to the breed. Pixies, luckily, have no such principles and this one has been buzzing her head off since she landed on my colleague's windshield.

The woman kneels beside the vampire, taking him for a fallen private investigator.

"Man, you are nearly gone," she murmurs as Vesper jumps up to rub back and forth on her bent leg, white fangs gleaming.

I know what Vesper is thinking—she is hoping my hard-won assistant will trip over her onto her master and become instant fang bait.

He struggles, feeling the temptation, and manages to whisper, "Stay away."

"No can do," the woman says. "The pixie blabbed all. The name is Delilah Street. I am a paranormal investigator who has met a daylight vampire. I know your more-evolved type is mortally harmless to humans. We need to get you somewhere private."

He struggles as her hand reaches for the claw dart in his chest.

"Bespelled!" Wasp-Wing whines a warning, hovering over Delilah Street's fingers.

"No problem," she says, jerking out the claw as if it was a mere thorn. "What is your name?" she asks the vampire.

His body still twitches from the stake's removal.

"Damien Abbott," he gasps. "You planning my gravestone? A daylight vampire will not rise again, never fear."

"You had better rise now or you *will* die, and these cats and the pixie seem unhappy about that, which is good enough for me. My blood is a bit off, human docs tell me, but I am the only oasis you have got going, pilgrim. Can you take just enough to walk a few feet?"

"I am stronger unstaked, but my control is shaky."

"I will have to trust it. I have never been vampire-bit. A minor withdrawal does not put me on the road to turning, Damien, but just a sip, pretty please."

"You are not my client."

"No, *you* are *mine* now." She bravely extends a bare wrist to his lips. "As the Wicked Witch stepmother said to Snow White, whom I happen to resemble, "Come, bite.""

She is right. In the faint light I see her skin is almost as pale as the vampire's and her hair as dark. I never thought I would live to see a smart dame inviting potential disaster, but I have heard Miss Delilah Street is the nervy type. I position myself to take a big chomp out of the guy's private parts if he should over imbibe, and I can see his eye-whites glisten as his gaze shifts to the threat I pose.

Miss Delilah Street shudders a pixie shiver and then all is silent and still in the alley until Damien jerks his head aside.

"I did not feel a thing," Miss Delilah says.

"I secrete an initial drop of anesthesia."

"In fact," she adds, purring a little like Vesper, who is now kneading her master's arm, "you remind me of my daylight vampire acquaintance, who is quite a sexy guy."

"I secrete an aphrodisiac as well."

"Oh." She jerks back, then moves behind him and bends to get an arm under his shoulder. "Upsy daisy. Does my blood have any special effects?"

He lurches upright and actually cracks a smile. "It is a bit on the effervescent side. You enjoy your Champagne, Delilah?"

"I am the Cocktail Queen of the Inferno Bar from time to time," she quips. "I invent 'em more than drink 'em. Come on, you had the smarts to get darted just feet from the back of Wrathbone's Bar. I called ahead for a private room."

"You are confident. What about—?"

"The cats are following."

"No, the , the —"

Miss Delilah Street looks down at me. Wasp-Wing had curled back into her ball, which I had rolled shut. Right now the lot was in my mouth, in my live prey carry, which would not dent a cotton ball.

"Who do you think told me your location? Handy little thing."

"Wasp-Wing is my version of a cell phone, and Vesper's companion."

"Worry not. Your pocket-rocket pixie is safely stowed. Midnight Louie's custody is the safest place for it."

"You know this alley cat who has designs on Vesper?"

"Yup. He is a primo private eye, although I am surprised to see him walking on the wild side down here. He is not as young as he used to be."

I beg your pardon! I bare my fangs. But Miss Delilah Street is too busy planning her next move to pay any attention to mine.

"Get inside," she tells the temporarily revived vamp, "where I can nail the dart-thrower and save your undead life."

**Miss Vesper pauses** on the threshold, flaunting her fantail in my face to bring me to a sudden stop.

"So you are a notorious figure in the Overworld," she says.

I sigh and let Wasp-Wing's carrier down to roll into the room beyond.

"I do cut a wide swath," I say, striking a duelist's pose with my foreshivs extended.

"All you have done for my master is hang around *me*."

None are so unappreciated as the subtle. I step aside to permit the lady to enter first.

Wrathbones is a rather rowdy venue, I have heard, with armed skeletons decorating the walls and a clientele that runs from adventure-seeking tourists to celebrity zombies to werewolf mobsters to vamps and narcs.

This room we have entered, however, is rather luxe, with an inner sanctum, i.e., bedroom.

"Perfect," Miss Delilah declares, ushering our wounded vamp onto the bed within. "You might as well husband your resources in your usual field of operations."

"I have only so many minutes before I will need more than your compromised blood to keep conscious, much less . . . viable," he warns.

"Relax," she tells him as Vesper rushes to claim what must be her usual spot on the bed. I well recognize the instinct. My Miss Temple has only one significant other (at a time; there are two vying for the prime spot), but that is another story in another place and time.

Poor Miss Vesper must share her master's accommodations with . . . several usurpers. I hasten to the anteroom and Miss Delilah's side. She has seated herself to scroll through our host's social register.

"Seven women," she mutters, "one for each day of the week, and all at staggered times. Six a.m. Thursday, nine Friday, noon Saturday, three Sunday, six p.m. Monday, nine Tuesday. And midnight tomorrow, Wednesday."

She eyes my attentive presence. "Our vampire is a creature of habit, which makes him easy to target. I wonder if daylight vampires ever actually sleep."

I settle on my belly, forearms wrapped and abutting in my "wise mandarin" pose. Any minute now I would be calling Vesper "Grasshopper". were she not reclining in the bedroom.

"What is today's nine p.m. client, Corinne, besides late?" Miss Delilah asks herself, and me. "Is she at their usual rendezvous? Or does she know she need not bother? Why not text her to come here?"

"Now," Miss Delilah tells me, "that done, it is high time for an interview with the vampire."

**I appreciate being** kept abreast, so to speak, of the proceedings, and accompany her back into the adjoining bedroom. Vesper reclines beside her enervated master, although the crimson velvet bedspread is my main attraction. I would look terrific on it and my black coat would add a formal touch nestling next to Vesper's dazzling white one.

Damien probably looks tasty to human females, with his white silk shirt open to allow the wound to heal, and his black-suited form long and lean against the plush fabric.

I assume Miss Delilah Street must be thinking the same thing, because I hear her catch her breath.

"Shades of the gentleman vampire known as Sansouci," she murmurs mysteriously.

"I had no idea the Sinkhole had places like this," Damien says lazily.

"Vegas has always sold seduction," she answers.

"You realize I need to get back on my feeding schedule soon. Your blood is strangely soothing and exciting at the same time, but I took only what I needed to get to a safe place."

"I know all that. One of your ladies is en route."

"My nine p.m.? Corrine? Good. She has a calm nature. No hysterics from her."

I can see Miss Delilah register that at least one of his ladies is hot-headed.

Speaking of hot-headed ladies, Damien lifts a pallid hand to stroke Vesper's little pink ears, earning a slit-eyed purr. Pitty-pat goes my heart.

Miss Delilah sits on the foot of the bed. I see Damien's shoes have been slipped off and he is in stocking feet, like Vesper and myself.

"Tell me about your clients," Miss Dee says. "I know their names and appointment times from your Blackberry."

He shuts his eyes to save strength to talk, and perhaps to picture the seven mistresses on whom his undead life depends daily.

"Corrine is a widow who deeply loved her husband and wants no other spouse. The Midnight hour belongs to Violet, a Goth girl who is dying to live the part. Dawn brings Petra, a career woman with no time for human love. Nine in the morning is Tess's time. She is an artist. Noon means I lunch on Suzanne, a retired nurse who enjoys ministering to the needy. At three, Nelda arrives for tea and sympathy. She has multiple sclerosis, but is doing well now. The ancients thought blood-letting beneficial for disease. Sunset falls when Vyrle comes. She is a chorus girl and finds our activity energizing."

Miss Delilah snaps Damian's Blackberry shut and rises.

"I will admit your nine p.m. appointment when she arrives."

"Corrine." He smiles, relieved. "What a lovely person."

It is hard to pull myself away from the vision that is a red-velvet reclining Vesper with her pink nose and ears and very sharp white teeth. I could certainly spare a little blood for a rendezvous with a hot tamale femme fatal . . . .

Miss Delilah shuts the bedroom door and pulls a Mama-san chair with a huge round rattan back against the wall and sits. It provides an impressive background for her white skin, black hair and morning glory-vivid blue eyes. She would make one gorgeous blue-eyed black cat.

"The only thing to do, Louie," she addresses me as I arrange myself formally at her feet, "is to put each of Damien's ladies to the test. I urgently texted them all to come here. We must find out where hatred hides behind their vampire-loving exteriors, because that surely was the motive."

Hatred of Damien? I wonder. Or someone jealous of his attachment to his other lady friends? Human emotions get so messy when it comes to sex. My kind avoids that sort of trap thanks to a little inborn thing called "heat."

The door to Wrathbones opens to admit a roar of laughter and the reek of booze, smoke and blood. In walks Miss Corrine. I see right away that Miss Delilah Street is dumb-founded. Me too.

Miss Corrine is at least sixty, which can mean well-preserved these days, but still silver-haired and sedately respectable. One would not imagine her in abandoned intimacy with a vampire, but life is like that and it takes a lot more to surprise Midnight Louie.

57

"Who are you?" Corrine demands suspiciously. "I know it is nine-thirty. I was not on time for my nine o'clock, but he was not there…"

"I am Damien's … agent," Miss Delilah says. "I am afraid that he has been injured—"

Corinne ingests a gasp of horror.

"—and he needs a full measure of replacement blood at once. Perhaps a client would be willing to… give all to save him. As you know, a future eternal life as a daylight vampire would not be insurmountable."

"Oh, no! How terrible. Poor Damien. He is a dear, but I have several grandchildren. Surely my usual allotment would help?"

"Not enough fast enough."

Miss Corrine glances to the closed door and shudders. "I am so sorry. I live for my grandchildren. They need me. Several are in half-vampire, half-human families. I cannot give them up."

"I quite understand. Would you mind waiting at the reserved table outside the door? Damien's other clients are arriving. One may make the ultimate sacrifice and save him. Or… he may wish to bid you goodbye."

"I do not know. . . ."

"Drinks, of course, are on the house."

"The others are coming? I know nothing about them. We have never met."

"Now is your opportunity."

It looks as if Miss Delilah Street knows females almost as well as Midnight Louie does. I have never seen a one who did not want to at least eyeball a romantic rival. Or maybe do her in. Or their common object of affection.

No sooner has Miss Corrine, the widowed grandmother, departed then another knock comes.

The entering woman wears an expensive navy power suit and high-heeled pumps. Her skirt and hair are short but sleek. She is a handsome forty-five but already consulting the Rolex on her wrist

"Petra, I assume," Miss Delilah says.

"The message said Damien needed me. That is s*ome* role reversal. I have had an amazingly long day. Damien knows I start at 7:00 A.M. and go until whenever. He is the only thing that relaxes me, but once a week is all the time or blood I can spare. What is the 'emergency?' "

"He is dying."

"Oh. Is that possible? He is, you know, immortal. And unbelievably durable in bed, I might add. Are you another client?"

"His agent. He needs an entire blood replacement. I am sure the woman who volunteers would find the intensity ecstasy."

"Impossible. My schedule."

"Would you pause for a drink at the reserved table outside, then? He would wish to say goodbye if none of his other clients can accommodate him."

Petra eyes her glittering watch. "'Other' clients. He never would say a word about them."

She also falls for the cocktail table gambit and leaves.

I rub against Miss Delilah's leg to express my approval as we await the next woman.

The bold knock announces a thirty-something woman sporting a long red braid down her back. Her tie-dyed leggings are turquoise and emerald under an oversized bat-wing tunic bearing the motto "Arty Party."

"Oh, gosh," Miss Tess Tampa says when told the situation. "Damien is the sweetest, sexiest thing and our sessions really free up my creativity. The whole point of our arrangement is no strings. A performance artist cannot be tied down to, like, rules. Vampires have lots of tiresome rules. Sorry."

"You did religiously keep the nine A.M. meeting slot," Miss Delilah observes.

"Nothing else was religiously kept once I got there, though." Wink.

News of the drink table has her heading towards it with a "Sorry" shrug I do not buy.

The following knock is tentative and the opening door admits a human version of Wasp-Wing, a petite woman with brown hair in a wispy cut.

"You must be—" Miss Delilah begins.

This one speaks too fast and too much to hide her nerves. "Nelda. I have never been to the Sinkhole before. It was . . . hard to find."

"That is the point. But you did it. You were brave."

"Well, for Damien. He has done so much for me."

"I hear your MS is in remission."

"Yes, my parents are so overjoyed. If they knew what I had been doing these past two years . . . I was so afraid. I mean, I never . . . before. But Damien is so gentle and kind. I feel like a new person each time." She blushed. "How can I help him?"

She listens to Miss Delilah explain, sinking onto the chair near the door.

"How," Miss Nelda asks, "could he go without blood for so long? I know . . . there are others."

"That is a very good question, Miss . . . ?"

"Livingstone. Nelda Livingstone."

"You came . . . ah, your usual appointment is at three p.m.?"

"Yes. We have tea and talk and . . . lots of time. Such a wonderful break in my day."

"And what do you do during your day?"

"I am a computer tech at the Inferno Hotel. I will have to change to the night shift now, though."

"Are you saying you are willing to give Damien all the blood in your body?"

Her hands twist on her lap. "To save his life, yes."

"It is an undead life."

"Oh, he is far more alive than most people I have met in my so-called 'real' life. Is he in there?" She rises and heads for the bedroom door. "I should start now. I know what it is to feel weak and like your whole body and mind are deserting you. I am very strong now."

"Yes, you are." Delilah Street manages to step in front of the determined young woman. "This must be done carefully, not impulsively."

"But why delay? His existence—"

"We must give all the clients a chance to volunteer."

"All?"

Miss Nelda seems stunned, as if she had forgotten the others. My sincerity meter registers one hundred percent. She thought only of Damien and their relationship, and had from the first.

Miss Delilah is not ready to end her serial interrogations, though.

"Nelda, you can finally meet the others at the reserved table beyond these rooms, share a glass of wine. The situation does not need to be addressed until, oh, midnight."

"But why wait—? I could at least start him on the road to recovery."

I rise to stand before Miss Nelda, who is giving Miss Delilah a push-to-push resistance.

"Damien's wishes must be consulted," Miss Delilah says.

"Oh." The idea wilts the slender young woman's starchy resolve. "You mean he might choose another to join him for eternity. I . . . I had not considered that. Of course. I will wait outside. Whatever he . . . Damien . . . wants. Needs."

She leaves in the same shocked condition as she had arrived.

"One," Miss Delilah says triumphantly. "She truly loves him. Whether it could turn the other way, I doubt. Yet strong love can breed stronger hate."

Me, I am not a huge believer in what humans call "love." Cupid is not my middle name. My usual stoic expression must appear dubious because Miss Delilah Street deigns to look down at me.

"I appreciate your adding your not inconsiderable weight to keeping Nelda's determined feet from heading right for Damien."

Another knock, followed quickly by a louder one. We peek out the open door to see two very different women arriving at once.

*Va-va-voom!* One is certainly my cup of sizzle on the hoof. The other is as different as she could be.

Ms. Goth Grrrl struts in first, almost as tall as Miss Delilah, wearing high-heeled black patent leather boots laced-down the back in scarlet. Her hair is a Bad Witch Glinda fall of artificial red, her stockings striped and her torso corseted.

"The name is Violet," she announces. "Where is my handsome vampy boy? I hear he needs some physical therapy and I am the gal to give it to him."

"I am his agent," Miss Delilah claims again. "And who is this?"

"I do not know," Violet huffs. "Some mundane broad."

"Young woman," the second lady answers for herself, "dressing over the top does not give you license to talk over the top. I am Suzanne. I am a nurse. And I can certainly minister to the needy better than you."

"Violet," Miss Delilah says, "you are the six p.m. client and Suzanne has the noon slot.'

"Whatever," Violet says with a shrug. "Damien loves me best. Show me to him and let the games begin."

Suzanne steps in front of the buxom Goth girl. She has curly brown hair and must be fifty to Violet's twenty-two but her wiry frame is steel and so are her gray eyes.

"Look and listen, Missy. Damien is not a bone and a hank of hair to be fought over. He is a sick man and, as a nurse, I am best equipped to help him. I always was."

"Interesting," Miss Delilah notes. "Suzanne, you always considered Damien ill and your relationship like nurse and patient?"

"For heaven's sake, the man has a blood disorder."

Violet rolls her eyes. "He is a *vampire*, baby. Get real. That makes him a sex machine. That is what you craved, not some namby-pamby nursing fantasy."

Miss Delilah takes them both by the upper arms. "All his clients cherished a fantasy Damien fulfilled in many different ways. The question is, will you give him all your blood and your mortal life to keep him meeting with you, and the others?"

"Hey," Violet says, shaking loose. "I am in it for hot sex and the make-believe. Let *her* empty her veins; they look cold enough."

"Ah," Suzanne *hems* on the way to *hawing*. "My *real* patients need me with such a nursing shortage, and the hospitals do not even allow daylight vampires on their staffs. Conflict of interest. Sorry."

Miss Delilah keeps their upper arms in custody and gives them the joint bum's rush while I silently cheer her on. Miss Six p.m. and Miss Noon equally disgust me. Not even one tremor of concern for Damien. Or his bereft Vesper. Or little Wasp-Wing. Maybe they do not know about his dependents, but tough. I bet he knows about theirs.

"One more," Miss Delilah says, peering out the door at the assembled women. "And here she comes, I think. Last but clearly not least."

I am curious enough to jump off the side chair and peer through my temporary partner's bejeaned legs.

Miss Delilah probably brushes six feet in her stilettos, but she is wearing low-heeled mules now and the oncoming female is likely six feet barefoot. She catwalks through the door in an off-the-shoulder red spandex top and Capri pants. She strides into the room on wooden platform sandals that tie around her ankles. Her hair is a blond ponytail that falls to where her tail would start were she feline, literally as well as figuratively.

"Vyrle, the six p.m. appointment, I presume," Miss Delilah says.

"Who are you?"

"The name is Delilah Street. I am helping Damien with his condition."

"Which is?"

"Terminal."

"A dying vampire? That is a new one." Vyrle hungrily eyes the closed bedroom door. "I can bring him to life again."

"So can anyone who will sacrifice all her, or his, blood to Damien and live as a vampire forever."

"Not my ambition."

"What is your ambition?"

"To earn fifty thou a week at the Karnak Cleopatra spectacular show, and I am doing that. Damien was one of my daily pre-show energy-pumping techniques. And that alley cat is sniffing my shoes! *Scat!* Sultans have bid hundreds of thousands for a one-time onstage-used pair."

*Eeuw.* My nose retreats in haste. There are shoe fetishes, like some women's high heel collections, and then there are creepy shoe fetishes, which this lady's wealthy fans indulge.

Besides, I have learned all I needed to know. My first impression from her overbearing perfume has been confirmed by her stinky feet.

The nose knows. This Vyrle dame is the dart thrower, live and in person. All I need now is a way to tip off Miss Delilah.

But my partner seems to be following her own line of inquiry. "So you would not renounce all that fame and fortune to save Damien? If you were a vampire you would get to bleed your admirers physically as well as financially."

Vyrle snorts her disdain and tosses her pony tail so haughtily I am tempted to leap up, tangle my shivs in it and pull hard.

When Miss Delilah mentions the reserved table and the free drink while she checks Damien's condition, the Karnak high-kicker amazes me by accepting the offer.

"Excellent," Miss Delilah tells me, or the room, or just herself after Vyrle sashays out. "All our suspects are corralled for the denouement. Now to approach our would-be victim again."

Hot dog! As tragic as the situation could become, I will be able to feast on Vesper's beauty once more.

Inside the bedroom, Damien lies, the usual pale and wan.

Miss Delilah arranges herself on the foot of his bed. "We have a candidate for your full revival."

"My clients came when you called?"

"To a woman. Everyone. They are a varied bunch."

He smiles faintly.

"And some seem to owe more to you than you to them. Are you tamed predator or prey?"

"Neither, I hope. I am fond of all my clients, each in her own way."

"Well, one of them is not fond of you. Midnight Louie has tagged the dart thrower for me, and you."

I may swoon. I am actually being given full credit for my sleuthing powers. What a novel experience! I must work with this wonderful lady more often.

Damien frowns. "You know the motive?"

"Jealousy."

"How? I see them separately. They never meet."

"Now they have."

He winces.

"But none of that matters. I have found one who will happily give blood and be turned for you."

"That is amazing. I would never ask that of anyone."

"She volunteered."

"Was it Violet? I would think she would be thrilled by the opportunity."

"She was not, alas. The Goth stuff is a pose, not a true vocation."

"Vocation?"

"The word surprises you?"

"It is just an . . . odd way to put it."

"I never mind being odd."

"Then," he says, "it must be Corrine. A sad, lonely woman with no hope of a human romance after losing her beloved husband. She would make a loving daylight vampire."

"So you consider your role as therapy as much as a survival and sexual exercise?"

"There must be more than just sex for any relationship to endure, no?"

"I am asking what you think."

"I could not do what I do, give passion, if I had no compassion."

"Alas, not everyone is like that. Not every woman. But you will pleased to know that your secret enemy is not an ordinary woman."

"If Violet and Corrine are not willing to become vampire, it must be Suzanne. She is the soul of tenderness."

Miss Delilah Street smiles. "Your expectations do you honor, Damien, but then it is always about honor for you, is that not true?"

"What little honor one can find in these days," he mutters.

"Such an honorable man for a vampire. So methodical. One would almost say . . . canonical."

Can a vampire turn pale? At that moment Damien's blood-thirsty skin seems whiter than Vesper's fur, than the bed linen, than bone and fang.

"I may not have. . .long," he says. "Yet I find even this half-life too precious to lose."

"Cheer up." Miss Delilah Street is displaying a shocking amount of insensitivity to the dying man, even if he is vampire. "You have a savior, remember?"

"Must you put it that way?"

"Yes, indeed. I will end the suspense. She is Miss Nelda Livingstone—ironic last name, yes?—and she is wholly willing to give you every last drop of blood and die and live again as a vampire."

"Nelda! She has faced the most pain of them all! It cannot be Nelda. It will not be Nelda. I would rather perish."

"Then she will be condemned to a living death, for she loves you. I now see you clearly love her.

There is no reason you should not be joined in eternal matrimony."

"God, no!"

"God, *yes!*" Miss Delilah Street says, leaning so close to Damien that Vesper leaps up and hisses. "*What* were you, and *where* were you, when you were bitten into a vampire?"

His waxen hands try to ward off her burning blue eyes and biting voice. I recognize a fellow truth seeker at her most ruthless.

"It was long ago. Centuries," he says.

"When, Damien?"

"The twelfth century."

"You must have been young," she notes.

"Thirty-four."

"Where?"

"England," he admits.

"Where in England, Damien? You know you cannot lie."

"At Gracethorn Abbey."

"You were bitten at an abbey?"

"Yes."

"Turned there?"

"Yes!"

"You were a monk there?"

No words issued from his whiter-than-death face.

"Damien?"

"I was . . . the Abbott."

Of course, think I. Damien *Abbott*.

Miss Delilah Street jumps up. "Vesper. You, out. Midnight Louie, see to it."

We felines obey as one, as if demons were on our tails.

Miss Delilah, in fact, strides out hot on our heels.

She jerks open the door to Wrathbones, admitting the noise of merriment and anger and passion and debauchery.

"Nelda, you are needed inside. Quick!"

Miss Delilah slams the outer door shut and locks it after Miss Nelda comes running in, white-faced herself, straight for the open bedroom door, which Miss Delilah shuts firmly after her.

Then she unlocks and opens the outer door and approaches the nearby table.

"It is all right," she tells the assembled clients of Damien Abbott. "Thank you all for coming and your time. You may go now. We will be in touch. Damien will be fine."

Amid the buzz and wondering and questions, Miss Delilah retreats and shuts herself in with Vesper and me.

Even a hardened street sleuth like me has to wonder—or not wonder at all—what is going to happen on that red-velvet-spread bed.

Miss Delilah Street folds her arms over her highly sufficient chest and keeps an eye on the outer door. I recognize top-alert guard duty from when my mama used to take us kits out to learn the ways of the world.

I would not want to try to pass Miss Delilah Street right now.

**How she knows** we will get an unwelcome visitor, I do not know. Me, my shivs are already primed.

The door breaks open and shatters to nothing, filled by a fury straight from hell. The noisy occupants of Wrathbones fall silent and sit frozen behind it, as if caught in a huge glass ball, like Wasp-Wing. The hovering pixie shrills once and vanishes. Vesper growls like a tiger and stands shoulder-to-shoulder with me.

I eye our invader. It is Vyrle, only she is now seven feet tall and her hair is a floor-length cloak of fluttering, snapping, sparkling red and yellow and black flames that surrounds her figure and snarling elongated face—eyes, nostrils and lips slanted upward in an expression of evil incarnate.

The only recognizable thing about her are the telltale wooden platform shoes, currently sprouting sharp claws two inches long. I would not rub my muzzle there at the moment.

"I thought you got the message," Miss Delilah Street says. "You are not welcome here."

"He is mine!" the deep yet eerily feminine voice tolls like a bell. "Mine."

"Not at the moment."

"Mine for centuries, stolen from me, from my palaces under the hill, from my court, from my company."

"History does not support your claim."

The creature's bereft cry creates a crack in the invisible glass ball of frozen reality  behind her. "He was almost mine, before a vampire gypsy turned him. I assumed a foul, stumbling, stinking form here and sought for two years to lure him to the Sinkhole, where my powers can flower. That human female is with him now and weak and soft and powerless."

"But I am not."

"You! You are nothing but a meddler."

Midnight Louie has been called such a thing before, by those who underestimated me. I hope that Miss Delilah Street is being underestimated too. I know better than to interfere. Sometimes it is wiser to be Zen than kung fu.

I notice something glitter at Miss Delilah Street's right wrist. The finest silver chain . . . Changeling silver. It could harm Wasp-Wing if not undercover and under control. Are Vesper and I going to be treated to a manifestation of the infamous silver familiar born from the long lovelock of the Inferno Hotel's albino rock star owner, Christophe? Who knows what powers he commands? Not anyone in Vegas.

"When meddling is successful in my world," Miss Delilah Street purrs at this horrific entity, "they call it 'case closed.' Get out of here."

A roar and shattering sounds echo all around us, Vesper and I cling together, clawing our shivs into the floor boards to stay put, our coats rippling. Nice.

"I am queen," our invader declares.

I see the fine silver chain on Miss Delilah Street's wrist is spinning and turning as if her bone and body were a loom. A glittering web is churning up her arm and shoulders and down her other arm, shining like the full moon.

Vesper and my pupils slit, as against the morning sunlight.

Vyrle's engorged furious figure spits thorn darts and daggers in a blinding blitz from the cold flames of her cloak of many colors.

Miss Delilah lifts her arms across her body and above her head unfolding lacy silver metal wings that look as delicate as cracked crystal. The queen's weapons stop, fall into nothing as her final wail peaks and fades and the glass behind her cracks from side to side and she vanishes into the bluster and rowdy noise and commotion that is again Wrathbones.

Nothing is left behind. Only her wooden platform high heels that I had rubbed my face against to draw attention to the thorn nubs that pocked them. The earthy odors I had scented on the dart impaling the fallen Damien reminded me of a certain tree all kits learn to avoid climbing because of its lethal claws of poisonous propensity.

Miss Delilah Street's powers of observation and deduction are all that I could wish for in a human partner.

Miss Delilah fists her hands on her hips as a silver tinsel rain evaporates into the air around her until she is bare of all visible jewelry.

"Good riddance! What a witch!"

She bends to pick up a shoe, running her finger along the newly clawed platforms.

"We are seeing her true 'sole'," she says with a wry smile at her pun. "These have sprouted acacia thorns like the one that skewered Damien. I had my suspicions when I removed the clawed dart from Damien, but you, Louie, detected the strong acacia scent of Vyrle's wooden platform shoes in their harmless guise," she tells me.

"Many plants have both benign and malign applications. This thorn-bearing tree is used in perfumes, medicines, and herbal preparations. It is also protected by the Fey, who can use its poison qualities, as you sensed. You and I and little vampire Vesper have just the met their Dread Queen, Louie. I guess a cat may look at a queen, after all, and rat on her too."

"*Ooh,*" Vesper purrs in my ear. "You are much better than you look."

That is more than somewhat promising.

**By now the** bedroom door has opened and the bedazzled lovers are creeping out.

"We heard a kind of mewing out here," Nelda says, brushing back her hair with a blush.

All that storm and fury. Were they dead to the world!

"Not to worry," says Miss D. "I was just shopping for a new pair of shoes." She waves one. "You will not be seeing the imposing and possessive Vyrle any more, Damien. You may be a vampire, but she was not of this world."

"She was the one who staked me with a claw?" he asks.

"Wooden, from the acacia tree."

"How did you know—?" Nelda asks, shuddering. "Also about my deepest secret feelings?"

"The deduction process was simple. If someone hates Damien enough to kill him softly and slowly, someone must love him enough to make that would-be murderer jealous."

"Of me? Or of my. . .companions," Damien asks.

"Of you all. Of us all, humans and unhumans. Vyrle is something else, something greedy and merciless. Fey. She almost had a handsome abbot in her power at Gracethorn Abbey centuries ago, but vampires are immune unless they venture into a former Fey touch-point, like the Sinkhole."

"Miss Street," he says, "Grateful as I am for your detective *and* matchmaking talents, you assembled all my appointments. I could have sipped from the innocent five you dismissed tonight. Even though Nelda's been turned, we will have to continue as usual anyway, and find Nelda clients in addition to mine."

"Call it a couple's practice." She shrugs. "Look, Damien. I go for long-term satisfaction on my cases. Even humans would rather drink deeply of life than sip it up in installments."

Damien remains silent, but I do believe he blushes. Fresh blood will do wonders.

Miss Delilah adds. "To keep from killing your victims, you gave up centuries of celibacy to become a daylight vampire. If you can't be celibate, you can at least have a life partner, and Nelda will benefit from being a daylight vampire. Your version can walk without harm in daylight by wearing sunglasses.

Research shows vitamin D in sunlight is good for people with MS, which is not a blood-related malady. Come on; you and Nelda have too much love and compassion not to share it with others. You *can* live on love."

Nelda nods. "I lived on two hours a week. Now I have eternity." She smiles seductively over her shoulder—nervous Nelda!—and returns to the bedroom.

Damien is torn, but lingers to question my partner more.

"I was pretty out of it, but what did you mean in the alley when you first arrived and said you 'brake for butterflies?'"

I give Vesper a lick and a promise to keep her attention and wait for the Divine Miss D to answer the vamp. I have been wondering about that myself.

Miss Delilah Street smiles. "To understand, you need to know about Dolly."

"A friend of yours?"

"Sort of. She is four thousand pounds of shiny black Old Detroit metal and wears chrome like Mae West draped herself in diamonds."

"A car?"

"Oh, please. She is a 1956 Cadillac Biaritz cream puff I got at an estate sale when I was on scholarship in college. She can outrun a Porsche and outmuscle a Hummer."

"Rather like you," he says with his own smile.

Nice fangs. Shiny and white. I always admire a guy with good grooming.

"Maybe. Anyway, when your messenger pixie, Wasp-Wing, came barreling straight for me and my 'Changeling silver,' on the Strip, she got caught in Dolly's slipstream and almost crashed on the windshield, except that she looked like butterfly, and I always avoid hitting them."

"You have my thanks, but I remain curious as to why."

Miss Delilah folds her arms and cocks her head. I smell a reminiscence coming on.

"Before I found Dolly and could drive myself," Miss Delilah Street says, "I was on a road trip with some college classmates heading for an out-of-town basketball game. A monarch butterfly hit the windshield. It got caught in the windshield wipers, its wings totally intact. They fluttered there at sixty miles an hour, looking alive.

"I asked the guy driving to pull over so we could at least free it. The Monarch had to be dead, but those wings were so alive as they fluttered, so beautiful and miraculously whole.

"He would not even slow down. We would be 'late" for the precious 'game.' Sick at heart, I watched those wings flutter and kiss the windshield as if performing a dance just for me for forty damn miles."

"But the butterfly was dead," the vampire says. "Why would you care?"

"It was still beautiful, and so alive in its way."

"That story says something remarkable about you, Delilah Street."

"It says something remarkable about *you*."

He gets the point and nods. Humbly.

"I have secretly hated my lot in undead life all these centuries." the vampire confesses. "Even when I could convert in recent years to sipping human life rather than taking it. I divorced myself from feeling, as you had to while you watched, the sole attentive audience, while the butterfly wings did their fatal *danse macabre*. But you are right. The imitation of life is life in its way."

He turns to regard the doorway to Nelda. "I hated the idea of her losing and wasting her precious life on loving a dead thing, but you say love is immortal."

"I say to each his and her own," Miss Delilah Street answers. "Should I leave Midnight Louie with Vesper, or return him to his usual haunts along the Vegas Strip?"

"I say we should leave it up to them," he says with a smile while Wasp-Wing dances above everyone's heads in excitement like a butterfly, expecting many interesting future fetches.

I nuzzle Vesper's perfect pink nose. I say that Damien Abbott is one stand-up vampire.

Carole Nelson Douglas

# THE THIRD TALE

MIDNIGHT LOUIE
completes THE LIGHTHOUSE, a story fragment by
EDGAR ALLAN POE

"THE RICHES
THERE THAT
LIE..."

CAROLE NELSON DOUGLAS

**AUTHOR'S NOTE ON POE:** One of Midnight Louie's and my most unusual story assignments was for the small press Cemetery Dance's project, *The Lighthouse,* edited by Christopher Conlon.

**From Michael Matheson:**

"Found among Edgar Allan Poe's papers after he died (at 40, all too young) was an untitled story fragment with an intriguing preamble. Consisting of three short diary entries by a newly indentured lighthouse keeper, the fragment affords few clues about Poe's plot intentions. The assignment for the 23 contributors to this unique collection was to finish the tale by using Poe's language, themes, and predilection for curdling the blood.

"Perfection is a rare quality in an anthology. But even coming back to Poe's Lighthouse…Christopher Conlon's startlingly diverse homage to the works of Poe—using an exploration of Poe's (in)famously unfinished "Lighthouse" fragment as the crux (literal or figurative at the choice of the author) of each story—is still unabashedly pitch-perfect....

"And what happens once we look at the stories individually is even more astonishing: Each is nothing less than the primal beauty of iterative interpretation at play. "Because of the finesse of the writers involved, Poe's Lighthouse is exquisite in both scope and execution... And each is a stylistic world unto itself; which potentially owes as much to the excellence of Poe's work itself, and its enduring ability to inspire, as it does to the masterful story-telling exhibited by the writers in this anthology. . . .

"Carole Nelson Douglas' 'The Riches There That Lie,' subtitled 'A Midnight Louie Past Life Adventure,' is a delicious tongue-in-cheek narrative. For those who are unfamiliar with Douglas' Midnight Louie, as I confess I was before reading this story, he is described quite aptly in the preface to the story as a 'feline detective.' There's a devious (false) simplicity to that premise, which allows the story to unfold through the wonderfully skewed vantage only a cat's—a singularly erudite cat's—understanding could provide. Douglas' work also shows an abiding love of Poe's source material, capturing the feel of his work, and referencing several other of Poe's celebrated works, to create a sense of a continuing narrative through which her long-suffering, ever-seeking feline wends."

## POE FRAGMENT

***Jan 1 —1796.*** This day—my first on the light-house—make this entry in my Diary, as agreed on with De Grät. As regularly as I *can* keep the journal, I will—but there is no telling what may happen to a man all alone as I am—I may get sick, or worse... So far well! The cutter had a narrow escape—but why dwell on that, since I am *here*, all safe? My spirits are beginning to revive already, at the mere thought of being—for once in my life at least—thoroughly *alone;* for, of course, Neptune, large as he is, is not to be taken into consideration as "society". Would to Heaven I had ever found in "society" one half as much faith as in this poor dog:—in such case I and "society" might never have parted—even for the year... What most surprises me, is the difficulty De Grät had in getting me the appointment—and I a noble of the realm! It could not be that the

Consistory had any doubt of my ability to manage the light. *One* man had attended it before now—and got on quite as well as the three that are usually put in. The duty is a mere nothing; and the printed instructions are as plain as possible. It never would have done to let Orndoff accompany me. I never should have made any way with my book as long as he was within reach of me, with his intolerable gossip—not to mention that everlasting mëerschaum. Besides, I wish to be *alone*... It is strange that I never observed, until this moment, how dreary a sound that word has—"alone"! I could half fancy there was some peculiarity in the echo of these cylindrical walls—but oh, no!—this is all nonsense. I do believe I am going to get nervous about my insulation. *That* will never do. I have not forgotten De Grät's prophecy. Now for a scramble to the lantern and a good look around to "see what I can see"... To see what I can see indeed!—not very much. The swell is subsiding a little, I think—but the cutter will have a rough passage home, nevertheless. She will hardly get within sight of the Norland before noon to-morrow—and yet it can hardly be more than 190 or 200 miles.

***Jan.2.*** I have passed this day in a species of ecstasy that I find impossible to describe. My passion for solitude could scarcely have been more thoroughly gratified. I do not say *satisfied;* for I believe I should never be satiated with such delight as I have experienced to-day... The wind lulled about day-break, and by the afternoon the sea had gone down materially... Nothing to be seen, with the telescope even, but ocean and sky, with an occasional gull.

*Jan.* **3**. A dead calm all day. Towards evening, the sea looked very much like glass. A few sea-weeds came in sight; but besides them absolutely *nothing* all day—or even the slightest speck of cloud...Occupied myself in exploring the light-house... It is a very lofty one—as I find to my cost when I have to ascend its interminable stairs—not quite 160 feet, I should say, from the low-water mark to the top of the lantern. From the bottom *inside* the shaft, however, the distance to the summit is 180 feet at least:—thus the floor is 20 feet below the surface of the sea, even at low-tide... It seems to me that the hollow interior at the bottom should have been filled in with solid masonry. Undoubtedly the whole would have been thus rendered more *safe:*—but what am I thinking about? A structure such as this is safe enough under any circumstances. I should feel myself secure in it during the fiercest hurricane that ever raged—and yet I have heard seamen say occasionally, with a wind at South-West, the sea has been known to run higher here than any where with the single exception of the Western opening of the Straits of Magellan. No mere sea, though, could accomplish anything with this solid iron-riveted wall—which, at 50 feet from high-water mark, is four feet thick, if one inch… The basis on which the structure rests seems to me to be chalk….

***Jan 4.*** [Here, Poe's manuscript fragment ends.]

# The Riches There That Lie

## *A Midnight Louie Past Life Adventure*

### by

### Carole Nelson Douglas

*There open fanes and gaping graves*
*Yawn level with the luminous waves*
—"The City in the Sea" by Edgar Allan Poe

**The nights in** these northern lands always smell of the sea. Tides creep in and out like assassins and bring death on every swell, with every hoary breath of salt air.

I am not a scavenger. I kill, yes. I eat what I kill. Sometimes I fence with Death. I am a skilled sword wielder and was known as a fearless blade in France before the Fall.

The fall of Monsieur Guillotine.

Louis of the Slashing Stilettos, I was called. Louis Noir. Louis de le Nuit. Sometimes Minuit Louis.

It is true that I have a famous ancestor. Does not everyone? The valet to the Marquis de Carabas was a clever, calculating dandy in his time, with his white whiskers and cravat, pale aristocratic gloves and swashbuckling boots... He served his master well.

I have never had a master. Nor a mistress. I go where I will, and I willed myself away from Paris, *la belle cité* turned *abattoir* during the Terror. Death is necessary to every life. Slaughter is not.

Not every nobleman in France died during that terrible year when terror officially reigned from 1793 to 1794. Some fled. Some even saved something more than themselves. Still, most lost everything: family, title, wealth, self-respect, life.

I carry my family, title, wealth, and self-respect on my back, in my skin. My kind are known for having many lives, most of them secret. We walk alone and if you would abuse us, beware. At the least, we will leave you to your own mean skimpy souls. At the worst, we will take our revenge in our time and our way and it will be...unpleasant.

So I sojourn here the for year of 1796, in Norland, in a cold climate among a cold northern people. Still, from the cold North Sea come the silver-scaled fish, the angel-feathered birds, and the furtive rats that a fellow like me can do well by.

I am a gentleman of the road by nature and make the most of wherever I find myself. Still, I long for more genteel places and climes and am thinking of so arranging it when I happen by a tavern on the Eve of the New Year to find two richly attired men conspiring in a foul alleyway nearby.

Now, nothing attracts my attention like the odd little movement in the odd little byway. Naturally, I draw my dark warm cloak close and move forward on velvet shoes. I become one with the dark wall behind me and perk my ever-sharp ears. And listen.

"He is half-mad but still too canny to reveal the hiding-place."

"Not even for the love of Marianne?"

"He has her love, and knows it. By that we may trap him."

The speaker puffs on a large-bellied pipe that has not been scrupulously cleaned. I am myself fanatically in favor of the scrupulously cleaned and nearly choke on its rancid fumes. But I manage to keep quiet.

"Still, Orndoff," says the other, "you have nothing until he tells you all."

"He must be reduced to desiring that state above any other."

"How? Love? That is a delusion. And Marianne will not help you. She believes she loves him too."

I must agree with the latter gentleman about delusion. Although love comes in heat, it departs in spats and hisses and chilled blood and is more fuss than it is worth, to my mind.

"We have demanded he fulfill a quest. He still clings to the notion of his noble family, though La Guillotine has harvested them noble head by noble head. He is a man horrified and lost, alone. He will soon long to do as we wish."

"So you send him…there?"

"Indeed. He goes willingly, claiming the solitude will only serve to settle his soul of past horrors before it revives to fasten on another and saving soul, my foolish sister's. Save his soul! My man, the solitude of the lighthouse will destroy it! But not before I know what I must. Then I can rid myself of my sister elsewhere for a handsome dowry and still hold the last wealth of the Le Martines. which is rumored to be a fortune in jewels smuggled out of France."

"When does he depart?"

"Tonight. On the cutter."

"Willingly?"

"He's been told that a year alone at the lighthouse is the only way to the hand of Marianne. That he will return to bliss on January 1 of 1797. A man of his station is prone to idealistic quests, and something in him seeks self-destruction, though he knows it not."

"You can play him thus and still expect his fortune?"

"He will blather what I wish to know to the sea otter and merman before I am done with him. The Lighthouse

has a blasted reputation. Three men manned it together before, and all left utterly mad. The lighthouse harbors more darkness than light. I know; I inspected the place after the last keeper had been taken away, shaking and muttering to himself. This French milksop will leave begging us to take his fortune off his hands, wherever he has hidden it."

Fortune. *Hmm.* I do not care for worldly goods but where two men conspire to acquire a third man's wealth, there are others equally as eager that he keep it, including the victim. Perhaps he, grateful, would offer me comfortable passage to Spain or Portugal... or even the New World.

"Away, vermin!" the man with Orndoff shouts, having spied my svelte form. He aims a boot at my head, but connects only with the sudden breeze left by my retreating black plume, my cavalier's symbol of honor and grace, my panache. My ancestor the Marquis' valet would be proud.

**Finding the cutter** in question is kit's play. Few small vessels venture out in this bleak season.

I am aboard, unseen, before you can snap a mackerel's tail.

The man under discussion is soon after escorted on board by a cloaked and somewhat tear-sodden damsel and the two men I had overheard in the alleyway.

He is a slender, morose man, with handsome features and a pale broad forehead that speaks of intellect even as his haunted eyes scream a horrific history.

"Not a year!" the young woman cries, clinging to his arm.

"Your brother so decrees. Don't fret, Marianne. I'll spend that year strengthening my soul and will return rinsed clean of all the horrors of Paris, a fit man to be your husband."

"You are fit now, Armand!"

He straightens. "I have been challenged. I am a Frenchman still. I will face the field of honor."

Fine sentiments. Still, he could use a bit more starch in his ruff.

A shadow swallows the gangplank as a last passenger boards. A dog! Large, black, the kind that loves water and game. He wears a thick black leather collar, the poor fool, and grins happily at the circle of humans around him, no more aware of who is villain and victim than a starfish would be.

I suppose the world has its uses for the inferior breeds, but not I.

"Neptune." Armand places a thin scholarly hand on the dog's great black head. "You see, Marianne, I will have this noble beast for company at the lighthouse."

*Hah!* I wish I could unsheath my stilettos and show poor Armand one of my kind in action. Yet he is right. He shall have the company of a "noble beast" at the lighthouse. I have taken a dislike to Marianne's scheming brother. I have nothing better to do. A fortune is at stake and the air reeks of fresh fish-belly, so... *Adieu,* Norland.

**The cutter is** a thirty-foot two-master with six oarlocks, thus offers scant room for concealment. Luckily, we leave at eventide so the dark, always my greatest ally, soon falls. And there is much business with the sails. I crouch in the shadow of the water-keg and keep my ultimate extremity well wrapped around me.

And why should a lighthouse lay a day and half's journey from shore? This I ask myself as the night wears on without any sign of making land. Neptune whines in the way of his kind in the stern, huddling beside his master near the rudder man. I cling to my hidden niche in the bow, soon regretting my impulsive adventure at sea, for the swells grow higher than the half-timbering on a London house. (I am a well-traveled sort).

Dawn is but a glimmer on the wave tops when a black spike like a doomed vessel's last surviving mast looms ahead. It sits atop the rocky pinnacle of some undersea mountain range. I fear for our craft's keel, but shortly thereafter a grappling hook snags on a sharp outcropping. Armand and portmanteau and overgrown puppy-dog are as much flung ashore like waves as landed.

I must remain while the oarsmen wallow the cutter in the choppy waters near this so-called landing. At last, as the sunlight slants over the water, the crew's backs are all to me, and Armand and Neptune have vanished into the dark needle of the lighthouse with its large, vigilant open eye at the top.

I make a mighty leap, for below me yawns a bitter patch of boiling black water. My own natural grappling hooks snag a lip of rock. I struggle onto the projecting shelf, brine stinging my eyes and matting my best black velvet coat.

Ah. I struggle upward and feel a bit of the sun glancing off my distinctive white whiskers. I am on the lighthouse rock unseen, and there must be victuals enough within to supply a man and dog for a year. And where there are victuals, this is food for Minuit Louis. (Pronounced, in the French fashion, and sounding like my kind's midnight serenades, *minoo-ee Loo-ee*.)

I do not expect to hear my name spoken in some time, but solitude is something I cherish as much as Armand. Nor do I expect us to be as alone in this locale as Armand thinks.

**What a forbidding** place! In outer shape it reminds me of a windmill in Holland, except it is topped with a lantern that beams by night like the North Star fallen to land.

Inside it resembles what I imagine is the interior of a certain chess piece, the only inanimate piece on the board, the cornerstone before play begins, the rook.

I had hoped for some peace and quiet on this remote outpost surrounded by dark waves of bottomless water. I was optimistic.

Armand, it seems, is a diarist. He mutters as he writes. He speaks to Neptune, which perhaps explains why such an inferior breed is a favored companion of loquacious Man. In fact, this serves my purpose well, which is to learn all I can, including the location of the jewels Marianne's brother so lusts after.

"Thank God for De Grät," Armand often mutters. At first I mistake the phrase for something other than a name, as in "Thank God for the gout." (Although why one would is a mystery.) Then I thought it might be "the grout," a reference to the cement with which Armand sealed away his family jewels. But, no it is clearly a given name even odder than my own.)

"How annoying, Neptune, my friend," Armand says, "that a first family of France must be reduced to begging De Grät for a cynosure on the loneliest site in the North Sea. Only the last man to do so finally put an end to all the sinister rumors, Marianne's own brother. Can I but duplicate his feat, no one, least of all he, can any longer contest my right to her hand, for I have readily won her heart."

Neptune pants at the appropriate places and whines at others. What a consummate player!

"I will survive this exile and thrive, my canine friend. Not only that, I will produce a book that will tell the world of the vile hypocrisy and violence of France's so-called Revolution.

"The year will fly, my faithful dog."

This I doubt, for I doubt that Orndoff will wait a year before claiming Armand's treasure. But how will he accomplish this, that is the question.

**Three days aboard** this wave-lashed rock and already I am impatient to cross swords with Orndoff again.

There is food aplenty, thus plenty of moving meat for my palate…mice, rats, even a company of crabs that have somehow infested the tower.

The place lacks sunlight and architectural interest, though, and I most miss sufficiently soft window-seat pillows. I cannot share the bed, for Neptune snores and would awaken and growl should I come near anyway. Already he snuffles along my trail, suspecting yet never glimpsing my presence.

I wonder if, when Neptune visits the rocks outside to do his daily doggish duty, I could lure him into the sea and the longest paddle of his life. No, without him Armand would not be so vocal. And, I confess, I cannot read the long, looping handwriting of Armand's diary and his so-called book, although I have tried. I suspect this may be a boon. He is of a gloomy, nervous disposition, and is haunted by acute hearing that imagines groans and creaks and rasps and scuttling everywhere. No wonder! The stone lighthouse is tomblike in its way.

Our situation is thus. We reside in a long, vertical tunnel of 160 feet, or an incredible twenty stories, like a cathedral tower. It is a sort of echoing, attenuated bell that narrows up to the mirrored chamber at the top, where looking glasses circle around like a company of ghosts to reflect the lantern light fed by sperm oil into a mighty beam visible from several leagues away. I envision the mighty leviathan of the deep hunted and slaughtered and carved like liquid ivory and squeezed into lamp oil for a thousand small and large lights.

The world is composed of predator and prey. Orndoff and I are predator. Whale, Armand, and Neptune are prey. It will be interesting to see who comes off this rock alive. I, of course, intend to be the last to know…the last alive.

From the lighthouse's ground-level interior, an iron staircase spirals upward beyond view, like a giant interior screw. It rings, and trembles, when Armand and Neptune make their nightly circuitous journey upward to feed the monster lamp more oil from leviathan's belly. Armand constantly adjusts the wick so that the mirrors do not reflect only smoke, and so that an earthbound star blinks far and wide to ships that would wish to avoid this treacherous spot of hidden rocks. No worry. The Devil himself would detour around it.

Small chambers surround the broader base of the lighthouse: pantry, bedroom, study. These are the more comfortable living areas I must avoid or else betray my presence.

There is yet more to the lighthouse, and more than there should be.

Armand, a sensitive man, has noticed "the echo of these cylindrical walls."

I do not believe for a moment that they are echoes. But, then, I myself have acute hearing, even more so than the dog, who relies overmuch on his large, snuffling nose.

**Armand spends his** spare time aloft, viewing the sea and seagulls with the telescope, watching the ever-changing panorama of the water, sighting the occasional vessel, which steers wide of us.

He has remarked, however, that below the living quarters lie another twenty feet of empty space. The broad base of the lighthouse is hollow, a great wide cellar, in fact, carved below the surface of the surging sea.

"It seems to me that the hollow interior at the bottom should have been filled in with solid masonry," he muttered and wrote soon after his initial inspection. "Undoubtedly the whole would have been thus rendered more *safe*."

Only *now* this fact occurs to a refugee from the Terror? What I spy below reminds me of nothing so much as a dungeon. Or a torture chamber. It defies logic, Armand is right. And what defies logic is decidedly wrong, even evil.

When I work my sure-footed way down a series of rough notches on one rocky wall, I hear the echoes from above magnified into faint caterwauling (I should know) and yet masked by the louder swish of the water as it admonishes rock. I feel the sea's salty fists beating on this hollow foundation for entry. In a few hundred years, the saltwater will win.

However strong the iron-riveted walls above—four feet thick—the lighthouse rests, as Armand rightly notes in his diary, with some consternation, "on chalk."

What a creature of vanity is Man, that he builds pyramids on sand and lighthouses on chalk, and vessels that sail endless seas in the dark, and smaller ones that reduce leviathan to lamp oil, and guillotines and ever more modern mouse traps.

I myself prefer to catch my mice the old way, with tooth and claw and trickery. And so, I think, does Orndoff.

**"It comes!" Armand's** voice reaches down to the hollow beneath the lighthouse, where I keep weary watch, to rebound off the coiling iron staircase and up to the chamber of smoke and mirrors and light above.

"The southwest wind that can drive the waves higher here than anywhere in the world comes our way. Neptune!"

Inadvertently he calls upon the sea god but is answered only by a dog. A sea-dog. Dog backwards is god, but dogs remain backwards and are no god to rely upon.

"My God!" Armand cries, as the spiral staircase shudders in the sudden relentless pulse of waves that makes even the rock waver.

He rushes down. I see his small figure against the light that still beams high above. Armand reaches the main floor, where Neptune leaps upon him, whimpering with fear.

So much for sea gods.

While man and dog teeter there, before they can reach the false shelter of the surrounding chambers, a wave as large as an iceberg jolts the entire island we call home.

Armand loses his balance and plunges deep into the empty, below-sea level heart of the lighthouse.

"Marianne!" he cries, as if her name might save him.

Neptune looks down from above, canine forehead wrinkled. His senses tell him pursuit is futile. His loyal heart tells him he should act.

From my perch on the notched stone wall, I watch Armand flail in the perhaps eight feet of foaming water that has kept his plunge from being fatal.

Now he is caught in a small artificial maelstrom, however, whirling around to bash against the rocky walls.

He will not die but he will be bruised to death, in time.

The sea, following hidden floodgates beneath the core of the rocks, washes in. Sea snakes, brown and leather, twine Armand's thrashing limbs like bonds.

He struggles to stay afloat, to breathe. He no longer calls on God or Neptune.

There are two possible endings: he loses strength and dies. Or he survives, a shadow of himself and as a shadow is retrieved by Orndoff when the storm slinks off. And in that maddened state he is interrogated and stripped of his past and his love and is killed, in the end, by something much less majestic than the sea.

And then there is the third ending, which I myself will contrive, for I like to write my own story and am ever contrary and independent of unwanted collaborators.

**First I must** clamber up the slick rock staircase to the first level. There I must persuade Neptune, by nature a retriever, to retrieve his master and keep him afloat.

Persuasion alone will not accomplish this. I lash his rear with a full complement of my blades.

He is screeching, over the edge and splashing below, in an instant, paddling for his life. He is large and strong and born to water, unlike myself, who is small but wily and most uninterested in moisture apart from a tongue bath. His master catches onto his neck, gasping, "Marianne."

Most touching.

Still the water rises up and up, bearing the living and inanimate with it, including strange sea matter.

I quickly apply myself to finding any loose baskets I can push into the tide below as flotsam to cling to. Alas, Armand's diary is kept in such a basket.

I empty it and send the container below.

What to do with the scrawlings on foolscap Armand has left behind, containing many clues and premonitions of this sad pass, had Armand only been perceptive enough to see them?

Using my sharp extremities, I roll the papers into a tight scroll and manipulate them into the long wide neck of an empty wine bottle. (Armand became partial to the Spaniards' Amontillado while marooned here. It seemed to assist the writing process.)

The cork is at hand but a hard thing to push into place. I am forced to position bottle and cork against the base of the iron staircase, assume a stern position at the rear, and wait for the waves to crush vibrating staircase, bottle, and my own firm stance together.

*Ouch!* But...*aha!*

I roll the bottle to the door the wind has blasted open, out onto the rocks, and push it into the storming sea.

The tides tend to Norland, for more than one sailor lost in these parts has ended up there with his corpse wearing seaweed for a beard.

At least Armand's journal shall reach land, if no one else here now will.

**I watch through** the nightly dark from above as the water oozes higher and higher until the internal waves swamp the ground floor. I retreat up the iron staircase, which sways alarmingly, for I am not one to get my boots wet. By morning the water has ebbed four feet below the ground-floor level. Neptune is still paddling, nose bolstered upon an adrift wicker basket. I have to give the breed credit for mute effort.

Armand's form is half-laid over a floating wine cask. Again the ever-useful Amontillado. I presume

Armand and Marianne will serve it on their wedding day.

For Armand is alive.

I wait for what I expect, a so-called rescue party that is quite the opposite. At length I hear grunting sailors, with scrabbling footsteps on the storm-wracked rock, then one set of boots stomping over the water-logged wood floor of the lighthouse.

Orndoff has come in alone, leaving his sailors moored to the edge of the rock. He shuts and bolts the wooden door behind him

He immediately looks down into the dark pool of seawater, as if inspecting it. Indeed, every violent storm must fill the drowning pool below. He eyes the apparent sole survivors, man and dog. Armand is a ghost of himself.

"Come, Armand," Orndoff shouts down. "Tell me where you've hidden my sister's dowry. Your family jewels, fellow! Tell me where you hid them and I'll throw you a rope."

He has no rope.

Armand rouses to the summons below, his eyelashes rimmed with sea-salt.

"Orndoff? You? Come to save me?"

"Save yourself. Tell me where the jewels are."

Armand blinks, still clinging to Neptune's neck and shoulders. "That is what concerns you? The jewels are safe."

"I'd hope so. Where?'

"In your sister's soul."

"Damn you! I want solid wealth, not romantic palaver. Speak or you drown here."

I take exception to this declaration.

I rush him, all my blades extended, slicing his breeches stockings from knee to ankle, both legs at once. The pain is sudden and paralyzing.

With a scream, he loses footing and falls below, thrashing in the deep roiling water. Like most men and cats, he does not swim.

He struggles to commandeer a floating basket, a piece of chair, to cling to and keep afloat.

Neptune, with the blessed possessiveness of his breed, snarls and snaps, producing a growl to shake the rocks. *Good boy!*

Orndoff flails, and fails to support himself in this most treacherous of elements.

He sinks, rises, screams. Sinks again.

The sailors storm the door with a mighty banging, and run in as I ebb into a discreet shadowy corner. They crowd to the pit edge to study the man and dog clinging to the wreckage.

And then they back off, not wanting witnesses to their complicity. I hear the cries from outside as they scrabble away from this accursed rock like crabs evading the waves of a beach and finally raise sail and oar to depart.

Man and dog rock on the bosom of the deep, filtered through a rocky chamber. I can do nothing now but watch.

In a few hours, the waters withdraw, marooning them both on raw piles of flotsam…and the body of Armand's would-not-be brother-in-law.

**Forced to make** myself known at last, I cannot say I am greeted with the credit I deserve. Yet my howling at the side of the pit leads Armand to discover the rugged way up the rock wall I had used. He collapses at the top, staring down upon a marooned Neptune as the crabs scuttle in to feast on the pale flesh of Orndoff.

The ebbed water has left the pit's bottom resembling some graveyard of the deep. Human bones have drifted in through the gratings now visible where rock-cut floor meets rocky sides.

One can now make out the rusted manacles bolted to the rocks. This area was a dungeon or torture chamber in times past. Orndoff adapted it to his own uses and, no doubt, would have treated Armand to that vile use had the storm not come unannounced and flooded the locks that, again no doubt, could be controlled by some fiendish hidden machinery.

Perhaps Armand would have been subjected to the turn of the thumb screw that echoes the shape of the staircase leading to the lighthouse's bright-lit salvation atop, like St. Elmo's fire in the masts. Rescue above, slow death below.

Speaking of which, I see that Armand has become agitated into action. It takes him the better part of what daylight remains, but by cutting his sheets and blankets apart and using a piece of carpeting, he constructs a sling he can lower into the damp pit below. One end of the cloths he wraps around the solid iron upright of the staircase.

I do my part by batting a thick piece of cheese to land dead center on this lowered carpet.

Neptune responds in the usual canine way: he leaps upon the cheese and the carpet.

Armand begins to draw the free end of his homemade rope hand over hand like a sailor. Neptune's brown eyes show white as he senses himself lifted by the middle, but Armand clucks and soothes him. Frankly, the average dog alone, without a pack, can be a craven creature. Fear holds Neptune limp enough for Armand to slowly reel him up to the lighthouse's ground level. There it is a struggle to entice the exhausted and frightened dog to jump from precariously balanced sling to solid wooden floor. Armand's arms shake with effort, and sweat has made rat-tails of his unpowdered hair.

I must take the initiative again, and leap upon the sling to spur Neptune sharply in the flanks. His yelp echoes to high heaven, or at least the old lamp far above, as his claws scrabble on the wooden lip.

Armand releases the rope to grab the dog behind the forelegs and pull him to safety.

I am left to plummet pitward with the released carpet-sling!

Luckily, I have done some sea faring in my time. I quickly unleash my blades to climb the swaying rope contraption as it if were salt-soaked rigging.

I must admit to relishing Armand's heroic efforts to save the dog that had helped keep him afloat. Perhaps both these species are not as sorry as I had thought.

**We are all**, of course, abandoned to the rock and the lighthouse. Some of the foodstuffs were spoiled in the flooding. Still, I am able to hunt. I bring down some gulls and procure some fresh fish for Neptune to devour. As Armand gains strength, he finds food that had escaped the flood, enough to feed himself and Neptune, and me.

"Lucky cat," he calls me, stroking my head. "Lucky black cat."

I am not lucky. I am clever, like my esteemed ancestor.

In two weeks time another cutter nears the lighthouse rock. We all draw back in fear even as hope lifts in our hearts.

Armand finally unbolts the door to take a peek. Miss Marianne sits in the bow alongside the rudder man, in whose hand is an empty bottle of Amontillado.

"Armand!" she cries from the sunny, jostling sea. "We received your message in the bottle. Thank God you are safe!"

He leaps off of the cursed rock and into the rocking cutter to embrace her. "Safe indeed. I never want to be so far from land again."

"Alas, the sailors report that my brother was lost seeking you."

Armand returns her embrace, but elects to conceal Orndoff's true end. By the time anyone attempts to reside at this lighthouse again, Orndoff will be only a few pale bones drifting in and out of the grilles that lead to the sea.

"I shall never be lost again, Marianne," Armand declares, "for I have discovered that solitude is not what I wish or need. I see now that I must use the means I saved from the Terror to create a new life of honor and happiness."

Well, isn't that an ironic ending? I join Neptune in scrambling aboard the cutter before it pushes off and leaves us to a diet of raw seafood forever. We keep company in the cramped bow while Neptune attempts to lave my whiskers with a long, pink, revolting tongue.

So ends my time on the lighthouse. My only appreciative witness to this life-and-death adventure is stupid and mute, and the man whose life I preserved has eyes only for a female of his species.

**I decide that** just because I am forgotten there is no reason I cannot remain around for the wedding.

A few days before this hastily scheduled event, the betrothed couple share a fireside chat. Neptune sleeps with his large black head on his paws. I keep to the shadows, as always.

"The message in the bottle," Marianne tells Armand, "conveyed your loneliness and regret but not the danger of the storm. Why did you send it into the sea?"

This I cannot wait to hear.

"The storm waters inundated the lighthouse before I could jot down any more words. They swept the bottle away barely after I placed my papers within."

"It's a pity your family jewels were lost there."

Armand says nothing, but pats his thigh. Neptune shakes himself loose from sleep, lumbers up, and goes to his master.

As the huge dark head pushes between Marianne and Armand, she rears back, laughing but annoyed. "He is such a large dog, Armand. I hope that he will not share our bedchamber."

"He likes the fire here in the parlor. And a large dog requires a large collar."

This Armand now unbuckles, removing and turning it over. He draws a small dagger and slits the rough jute backing on the leather.

Into his palm drops a glittering array of gemstones in broken settings, emeralds, diamonds, rubies, sapphires, all of fine size and fire.

"Your fortune!" Marianne cries. "It is safe."

I now regard Armand's heroic rescue of Neptune as less inspiring.

Still, one of the sparkling crimson stones falls to the carpet and rolls under a chair.

I snag it in a bladed fist.

Passage, I think, to a warmer, dryer clime.

Perhaps to the south of France, where the descendants of the Marquis de Carabas still reside and appreciate a clever fellow of my persuasion.

I am as able to aspire to golden boots polished daily by seven mice (a different seven mice each day, of course) as my enterprising ancestor, who was purported to enjoy that privilege, and others even more delightful and far less wet than my adventure at the lighthouse.

## ABOUT THE AUTHOR
www.carolenelsondouglas.com

**Carole Nelson Douglas** is the award-winning author of 63 novels in the mystery/thriller, science fiction/fantasy and women's fiction genres. She has written the 28-book "Alphabet" Midnight Louie, feline PI, cozy-noir mystery series (*Cat in an Alphabet Soup, Cat in an Aqua Storm, Cat on a Blue Monday* etc.) and also Delilah Street, Paranormal Investigator, noir urban fantasy novels (*Dancing with Werewolves*) set in imaginative variations of Las Vegas: contemporary and paranormally post-apocalyptic. A new Midnight

Louie series in his Las Vegas, using some elements of Delilah's world, is planned.

Carole was the first author to make a Sherlockian female character, Irene Adler, a series protagonist, with the *New York Times* Notable Book of the Year, *Good Night, Mr. Holmes.* She has won Agatha and Nebula nominations and Lifetime Achievement Awards from *RT Book Reviews* for Mystery, Suspense and Versatility, and was named a Pioneer of Publishing. Her Midnight Louie novels and stories also won several Cat Writers' Association first-place Muse Medallions, including for "Butterfly Kiss" and "The Riches There That Lie". Carole is e-publishing her extensive backlist of novels and stories.

An award-winning daily newspaper reporter, feature writer and editor in St. Paul, Minnesota, she moved to North Texas to write fiction fulltime and was recently inducted into the Texas Literary Hall of Fame.

## ALSO BY CAROLE NELSON DOUGLAS

"Her fine Sherlockian novels and her Midnight Louie books have turned her into a genuine mystery star. Pick one up and you'll see why."—**Ed Gorman**, co-founder of *Mystery Scene* magazine

## The *New York Times* Notable Book of the Year IRENE ADLER Series

*Good Night, Mr. Holmes*
*The Adventuress*
*A Soul of Steel*
*Another Scandal in Bohemia*
*Chapel Noir and Castle Rouge (Jack the Ripper duology)*
*Femme Fatale*
*Spider Dance*

## The DELILAH STREET, Paranormal Investigator, series

*Dancing with Werewolves*
*Brimstone Kiss*
*Vampire Sunrise*
*Silver Zombie*
*Virtual Virgin*

## The SWORD & CIRCLET and TALISWOMAN High Fantasies

**Irissa and Kendric**: *Six of Swords, Exiles of the Rynth, Keepers of Edanvant, Heir of Rengarth, The Seventh Sword*

**Alison and Rowan:** *Cup of Clay, Seed upon the Wind*

Carole Nelson Douglas

## The MIDNIGHT LOUIE Feline PI series

CAT IN AN ALPHABET SOUP

AQUA STORM
BLUE MONDAY
CRIMSON HAZE
DIAMOND DAZZLE
EMERALD EYE
FLAMINGO FEDORA
GOLDEN GARLAND
HYACINTH HUNT
INDIGO MOOD
JEWELED JUMPSUIT
KIWI CON
LEOPARD SPOT
MIDNIGHT CHOIR
NEON NIGHTMARE
ORANGE TWIST
HOT PINK PURSUIT
QUICKSILVER CAPER
RED HOT RAGE
SAPPHIRE SLIPPER
TOPAZ TANGO
ULTRAMARINE SCHEME
VEGAS GOLD VENDETTA
WHITE TIE AND TAILS
ALIEN X-RAY
YELLOW SPOTLIGHT
ZEBRA ZOOT SUIT

CAT IN AN ALPHABET ENDGAME

*Cat in an Alphabet Soup*
*Cat in an Aqua Storm*
*Cat on a Blue Monday*
*Cat in a Crimson Haze*
*Cat in a Diamond Dazzle*
*Cat with an Emerald Eye*
*Cat in a Flamingo Fedora*
*Cat in a Golden Garland*
*Cat on a Hyacinth Hunt*
*Cat in an Indigo Mood*
*Cat in a Jeweled Jumpsuit*
*Cat in a Kiwi Con*
*Cat in a Leopard Spot*
*Cat in a Midnight Choir*
*Cat in a Neon Nightmare*
*Cat in an Orange Twist*
*Cat in a Hot Pink Pursuit*
*Cat in a Quicksilver Caper*
*Cat in a Red Hot Rage*
*Cat in a Topaz Tango*
*Cat in a Sapphire Slipper*
*Cat in an Ultramarine Scheme*
*Cat in a Vegas Gold Vendetta*
*Cat in a White Tie and Tails*
*Cat in an Alien X-Ray*
*Cat in a Yellow Spotlight*
*Cat in a Zebra Zoot Suit*
*Cat in an Alphabet Endgame*

Delilah Street five-story anthology